LOSING THE FORBIDDEN

TRACY LORRAINE

*Lots of love
Tracy Lorraine*

Copyright © 2019 by Tracy Lorraine

All rights reserved.

No part of this book may be reproduced in any form or by any electronic or mechanical means, including information storage and retrieval systems, without written permission from the author, except for the use of brief quotations in a book review.

Edited by Pinpoint Editing

Proofread by Andie M. Long

Photography by James Critchley

Model George RJ

Cover Design and formatting by Dandelion cover designs

Andy and Amelia

PROLOGUE

Six years ago...

GLANCING over my shoulder at the house I grew up in, at the home where the people I love live, I know I don't have a choice. Walking away is the right thing to do.

I knew Nick, my stepdad, finding out about us would only end one way, but I really thought it would be with me in the hospital.

I never imagined this.

That vindictive arsehole knows exactly how to get what he wants. It's no different to how he wormed his way into my life. He wanted money and status, and my fragile, grieving mum was the perfect target.

Fire burns through my veins and my hands tremble with my need to find the motherfucker who's intent on ruining my life, but I know it'll be pointless. He's probably already got a plan in place for that.

Shoving my hands in my pockets, I force myself to walk away, to do what I need to do to keep the two women I love safe.

I've no doubt that the threats he just dished out were true. I've watched him ruin people before. He doesn't care about anyone, whether that's an employee or his own wife and daughter. He'll crush anything that gets in his way.

With one last look at the house my dad built with his bare hands, I tell myself that this isn't over.

I'll be back one day.

It might not be tomorrow, or even next year, but I will be back, and I will take what's mine.

Lauren included.

CHAPTER ONE

PRESENT...

"YOU CAN LEAVE NOW," I bark, sitting on the edge of my bed with my head in my hands. I wonder once again why I thought this was a good idea. Sex and alcohol have been the only things that help me forget. Even if it's just for an hour, or a night, the reprieve from my memories is worth it.

Only now, ever since receiving that phone call, nothing takes away the images of my old life running through my mind like a fucking movie.

"You know, you really are a fucking arsehole," the redhead says, snatching up her clothes from my bedroom floor and angrily pulling them on.

"I'm aware."

"I'm sure I could make it better, whatever it is," she purrs, sounding like a desperate slut. "I could release all that tension."

"Get. The. Fuck. Out." Normally I wouldn't be able to refuse an offer like that. I've used woman after woman in my attempt to forget, but none of them have even come close to *her*. None of them soothe the ache or the hole in my heart that's only been getting worse as the years have passed. Everyone around me might buy my act, but it's getting harder and harder to hide the real me.

I left the house that night with nothing but the clothes on my back, my wallet, and my phone. I had no idea where I was going to go or what I was going to do. With the amount of money sitting in my bank account, the world was my oyster. It's such a shame that the only place I wanted to be was the one place I couldn't stay.

I walked away, leaving my heart and soul behind, but I knew I didn't have a choice. The most important thing to me was to protect the two most important people in my life. My happiness was something I could easily trade for theirs.

I walked to the closest train station and got on the

first one that arrived at the platform, not giving two fucks as to where it was going. I just knew that I needed to get away. I needed to be as far away as possible by the time she realised I'd gone. I knew that if I was too close then the temptation to reach out to her would be too strong, but I couldn't risk putting her future in jeopardy like that.

My heart was already in pieces. I couldn't cope with seeing what my leaving was going to do to her. I truly believed that they'd be better off without me. It wasn't our time. I just had to hope that one day we'd have more luck.

That hope hung around for maybe a year at best. I found myself a new life and I was only living a lie to believe that we were meant to be. She'd have moved on. She'd be excelling at uni and making strides towards taking over the business that should have been mine. The thought of her moving on with someone else still makes my heart ache. It's been six years. She could be married with a couple of kids by now, but I can't shift the idea that it should be me. I should be the one she makes a future with.

I don't regret anything.

If I had my time again, I'm pretty sure I'd have done everything the same. I fell hard and fast for

Lauren, and I wouldn't trade that experience for anything in the world.

"Fucking hell." Pulling on a clean pair of boxers, I go in search of something to help squash the memories. Kristy...Kirsty...Kristal...whatever the hell her name is sure isn't helping, so I go for the next best thing.

Whiskey.

I unscrew the top and launch it across the room. What I really want to do is get my hands on something breakable, like someone's face, so the lid ricocheting off the wall and sideboard doesn't really have the same result.

Falling down on to the sofa, I bring the bottle to my lips and swallow down a couple of shots. I hardly feel the burn. I'm too numb.

I didn't have any expectations for what my life might be, but I've managed to create something close to a home here in this sleepy Devonshire town.

The train I got on that day took me to Exeter. I'd never been there before, but the idea of spending time by the sea held some kind of appeal to me.

I found a shitty bedsit and drowned myself in alcohol as I tried to figure out how I could have fucked everything up quite so royally.

All I did was fall in love.

THE NEXT THING I KNOW, there's crashing coming from the kitchen. Dragging my eyelids open, I wince as pain shoots through my head. I try to prop myself up on my elbow, but my head bangs and my stomach churns. Glancing down, I see the empty bottle of whiskey on the floor and groan.

"Morning, pisshead," Liv sings, a little too loudly, and I wince. She marches into the room with a bright smile and two mugs in her hands. "Here. I made it extra strong."

"Thank you," I mutter, sitting up and taking the steaming mug from her.

Her eyes are full of sympathy. Everything I've been trying to bury hits me once again. My chest aches and I fight to keep my breathing steady.

I told her yesterday about the phone call. She's the first person I've confided in about my previous life. In six years, I've managed to keep everything buried so deep that even my best friends have no idea. Both Dec and Liam have asked in their own ways about my past and my family, but I never once opened up. We've lived practically as brothers the past few years, and I know it's hurt them that I've kept so much of myself private. I never intended not to talk about what happened, but every time I even think about saying her name, all those old feelings, the devastation I felt as I walked away, hit me like a fucking hammer and I force it all back inside the box I've shoved it in so that I can attempt to live my life.

"When's the funeral?" Liv asks, dragging me from my living nightmare.

"Next week sometime. My uncle said he'd call back with more details once he has them."

She nods at me, an empathetic expression on her face. "You're going back before that though, right?"

Isn't that the million-dollar question!

Uncle Chris is the only person from my past life I've spoken to since the day I left. He's not really my uncle, just my dad's best friend, but he's treated me like a son from as early as I can remember.

When I left, I knew I needed some way of at least making sure both Mum and Lauren were safe. I needed to know that, with me gone, he'd keep his promise and they'd be able to live the lives they deserved, so I got in contact with him. Since Mum remarried, he'd kept his distance, but I knew they still spoke on occasion. He was the only one I trusted. We chatted quite often to begin with, but as time's gone on, we've drifted apart more and more. The moment I saw his name come up on my phone yesterday, a ball of dread sat heavy in my stomach. I knew he wasn't just ringing for a catch-up.

"Nick died last night." Those words have been on repeat in my head since the moment they fell from his lips.

My first feeling was one of pure happiness. That motherfucker was no longer breathing the same air as me. The world would be a much better place without a manipulative control freak like him. For the first time in as long as I can remember, my shoulders lifted, and I felt a little lighter.

That was until my next thought hit me like a truck.

Mum and Lauren.

My stepdad did a much better job than I gave him credit for of hiding the man he really was, because all these years later, Mum's still married to the wanker and Lauren continues to be in his life. If she had any suspicion that he had something to do with me leaving, I've no doubt she wouldn't have stuck around either.

But they're both still there, playing happy families.

I'm probably the only one who knows just how fucked up that reality is for all of them.

"BJ?"

"Shit, sorry. Uh...I've no idea if I'm going."

I can see the questions that are right on the tip of Liv's tongue, and I silently beg her not to ask them.

Up until earlier this year, my life in this seaside town consisted of my two best friends, one-night stands, and surfing. Then, Dec got himself whipped by his childhood enemy, quickly followed by Liam when he found the woman he'd always been searching for in the cute blonde staring at me with concern filling every one of her features. Of course, I was interested the first time we met her, but it soon became obvious that she only had eyes for one of us. She's too good to be kicked to the curb the moment I'd finish with her, anyway. She deserves her forever with Liam. Since she moved in, we've become close; she can see something in me, I think, something that everyone else either misses, ignores, or isn't brave enough to ask about. She's slowly breaking down the walls I've built up, and I'm terrified of what she's going to find if she manages to bring them all down.

Liv reminds me of the girl who captured my heart. They've got the same nature and a similar sharp wit. I've no doubt that they'd get on like a house on fire if they were to ever meet.

Sadness washes through me. Lauren would love it down here.

"What about your mum?" she asks, pulling me from my thoughts once again. Putting my mug on the coffee table, I drop my head into my hands. "Siblings?" The mention of siblings has me looking up. "What?"

I try to keep my expression neutral, but I can only imagine my heartache is clear in my eyes. "It's..." I can't say any more. It feels like the walls are closing in on me at just considering talking about her.

"It's okay. I was thinking about going for a walk along the beach. You fancy joining me? You can talk if you want...or not. I'm here for whatever you need, Ben." I hate the pain that hits my chest when she calls me that. I couldn't have been more relieved when I met Dec at Exeter uni and he nicknamed me BJ; every time I heard my real name, all I could picture was it falling from Lauren's lips.

"Let me shower, and I'll join you." Grateful to have something else to think about, I jump up from the sofa and attempt to wash away the stench of last night's alcohol.

The hot water does little to ease the tension

pulling at every one of my muscles. There's a war raging inside me, and I've no idea which side's going to win.

Do I go back, try to reclaim my place and go to the funeral? Or has too much time passed? Will I only cause more pain by going back? Deep down, I know what I want to do, what I need to do, but it's not just myself that I need to think about.

"I LOVE IT HERE," Liv says on a sigh when we stop by some rocks. Sitting herself down on one, she looks out to sea.

She might have sunglasses on, but I know the second her eyes flick to me. I try to ignore her attention, afraid she's going to try asking more questions.

"You said something to me once, and it stuck with me when I was going through all that shit with David and Griff."

"I did?" I ask with a laugh. I usually steer well clear of dishing out any kind of advice. I've already fucked up my own life; I don't need anyone else's on my conscience.

"*'Don't fuck it up. Life's a long time to live with regrets'*. And you're right. I'm not going to pester you about what you're going through. I know you'll talk when you're ready. Just think about those words. What will you regret more: going back or staying?"

"Fucking hell, Liv."

"You're welcome," is all she says before turning back towards the horizon, a small smile of victory playing on her lips.

CHAPTER TWO

"BEN, it's Chris. The funeral's going to be Thursday at one pm at the crematorium, and the wake is at The Crown. I understand your reluctance to come, but like I said before, I think your mum and Lauren could you use your support right now."

"Motherfucker," I shout, throwing my phone down on my bed and watching it bounce and crash to the floor. I was in the fucking shower when he rang, and now I've got the time and day of that cunt's funeral on my fucking voicemail, taunting me.

I spent the last few days fighting with my need to get in my car and drive to London to be with them. I've picked up my keys to go more than once, but something stops me every time.

They hate me. I know they do. He would have made sure of it. He told me he'd kill me for touching his daughter, and although I may still be breathing, I'm as good as dead to the two women I'd give my life to protect.

MY SOUR MOOD has had everyone keeping their distance from me—I assume at Liv's request. I can see in their eyes that they're worried about me, but they all know that sitting me down and demanding answers is going to get them nowhere.

Since moving here, I've made looking happy a full-time job. I've learnt all the tricks I need to convince everyone around me that my life's one big party. It's so far from the truth that it's not even funny. For whatever reason, Liv sees straight through it and she's starting to point things out to the others. I hate the sympathy in their eyes. Fucking hate it. It's one of the many reasons I've kept my past a secret.

Dec and Liam used to look at me with admiration. I showed the world that I had the perfect life: I had the looks, the brains, the women and enough money to not have to worry about where my next pay check was coming from. I've no idea how I got away without them questioning me for so long, but my time hiding from the truth is running out.

"Jesus, BJ, who died?" Dec asks the second he finds me sitting on the sofa later that evening.

Looking up at his concerned face, I can't help feeling grateful for Liv's discretion. She could quite easily have shared my bad news with everyone, but it seems she's kept my secrets from Dec at least. I'm sure Liam is another story.

"My stepdad," I mutter, pulling my eyes away from him in an attempt to hide the pain I'm sure is filling them.

"Fuck. Shit. I'm sorry, I didn't know. Liam texted to say we were taking you out tonight; I didn't realise—"

"It's fine, Dec. You weren't to know."

Falling down beside me, he's lost in thought and a ball of dread grows in my stomach. *Here come the questions.* "You know, in all the years we've known each other, you've never once mentioned your family. I didn't even know you had a stepdad."

"I know." I hate the guilt that fills me for keeping my best friends at such a distance all these years.

"I just kind of assumed you didn't have any, or that they're not worth knowing."

The silence hangs out between us, but when Dec

turns his gaze on me, I find the words just tumbling from my mouth.

"It's a bit of both. My dad died when I was a kid, but my mum married some arsehole who was intent on ruining my life." His eyes widen in surprise, but Liam's footsteps pounding down the stairs prevent him from asking any more questions.

Liam's eyes hold a sympathy that isn't usually there when he looks at me, and I can only assume that Liv has filled him in, hence the impromptu night out. "Are we ready? BJ hasn't had a shag in days. I'm worried it might fall off."

"You're a twat," I mumble, getting up and putting the cans I'd already drained into the kitchen. I can't really say too much; I deserve it after all the stick I've given him over the years.

"Aren't we going to Dec's?" I ask when I spot a taxi idling outside our house.

"We thought we'd be a little more adventurous."

Usually the prospect of a night out with my mates would excite me. They're getting fewer and fewer now that they're both loved up, but for the first time since meeting them, I think I'd rather spend the night at home alone as I continue to argue with myself about what I do.

Every time I've bumped into Liv in the house the

last few days, she's tried to convince me to go home. She knows I'm torn, and I think she's hoping that by reiterating what Chris said about Mum and Lauren potentially needing me, it'll make me go. I understand what she's trying to do. She thinks it's for the best. But she doesn't understand the clusterfuck that I'd walk into. I'm pretty sure me turning up while Mum and Lauren try to deal with their grief is the last thing they need.

When the taxi pulls up in front of the strip club, I drag Dec and Liam to every year for my birthday, I almost refuse to go inside. My head's too full of my previous life and *her* to have any desire to be surrounded by naked women. The prospect of possibly seeing Lauren again in only a few days has old cravings that used to consume my entire being returning.

Since getting that first phone call from Chris, every single memory I have of our time together is on fucking repeat in my mind. I see her out on the decking, surrounded by twinkling fairy lights that first night we spent together. I picture her laid out on a picnic blanket with the sun lightening her already fair hair. It's fucking torture. It's been six years; how I can still want her this badly is beyond me. She's just a memory now, but fuck if my body doesn't react as if she's right in front of me once again.

"What's wrong? You want to celebrate that that arsehole's out of your life for good, right?" Liam asks. I've barely scratched the surface with the details of my past life, but Liv's clearly passed on what a cunt my stepdad was. Dec's mouth drops open in surprise. It's really not like Liam to talk ill of anyone. "What?" he asks, his brows drawing together. "Liv said—"

"She was right. I think I described him as a waste of good oxygen. Come on, let's do this," I say with more enthusiasm than I feel. I've become a master at plastering a smile on my face and giving the impression that I'm okay, so I should be able to manage it for a night out. With my two best friends trying to support me the only way they know how, I can't exactly walk away from them.

Dec and Liam lead me to a table right at the front of the stage. It's where I always drag them when I bring them here, but today, it's the last place I want to be. Glancing over my shoulder to the booths in the back corner, I let out a sigh and pull out a chair. I don't want to come across like an ungrateful arsehole, but if I have to spend a few hours here, I'd rather be hiding in the shadows.

A tray of shots magically appears on our table and I waste no time in reaching for one and downing it.

Other than visiting the toilet, my arse stays firmly in the chair while Dec and Liam look at me like I've grown an extra head. It's not like me not to partake in everything offered in a place like this, but I already know it's not going to have the effect I usually crave. Sex and alcohol were my escape until that phone call. Now, nothing seems to quash the ache inside me and my desire for the only woman who's ever had a place in my heart.

I can only put up with the club and the concerned looks on my best friends' faces for so long. I down my drink and excuse myself, making it look like I'm heading to the toilets. Instead, I slip out the exit when both Dec and Liam are preoccupied with the girl up on the stage.

Sucking in a lungful of fresh night air, I feel like a pussy. I never leave a party. Well, *BJ* never leaves a party. I seem to be Ben more and more these days, and I'm not sure how I feel about that. The protective layers I've put around myself are being peeled away faster than I know how to deal with.

I don't bother calling a taxi. Hoping the long, peaceful walk will do me some good, I set off towards home. *Home*...I might love this place, but it won't ever truly be home. Home is where the heart is, and I left that in London a long time ago.

"Whoa, you guys are back early," Liv says, reaching for the remote to pause whatever she's watching when I eventually get back. Looking behind me for her boyfriend, her brows knit together.

"I couldn't stick it."

"This really is getting to you, isn't it?"

Falling down on the sofa, I drop my head back and scrub my palms over my face.

"I don't know what to fucking do," I admit.

She's silent for so long that I don't think she's going to answer. Her stare burns my skin, so after a few more seconds, I drag my head up and look at her.

"I think we both know what you need to do, Ben." Her voice is soft and her eyes hopeful. "As much as I want to demand you stay here because it's where you belong, I think we both know it's a lie. You're just using this place to hide. Whatever really happened is in the past now. He's gone. Whatever happened between the two of you, it's over."

"It's not really about him."

She nods at me to continue, and I try to swallow down the lump in my throat.

"It's my..." I cast my eyes away because, for how

supportive Liv is, I have no idea what she'll think to what I have to say next. "My stepsister. We... something happened between us." Blowing out a long breath, I continue to stare at the wall and will the tears that are starting to burn the backs of my eyes away.

Liv's quiet for the longest time. When she does eventually respond, my chest constricts painfully. "You really love her, don't you? Even after all these years."

I open my mouth to respond but no words come. The lump I was trying to get rid of returns as images of Lauren fill my mind.

"Jesus, BJ. You need to see her. You need to..." she trails off. She doesn't know enough about the situation to give advice, and I think she knows that. After casting her eyes away for a second in thought, she turns back to me and tries a different tack. "What's her name?"

"L...Lauren," I whisper. Pain twists my heart at just the sound.

"Pretty. I know you don't have to listen to me, and I don't really know what I'm talking about, but... don't waste any more time. I know you're scared, but what if she still feels as strongly about you as you do her? Don't regret not finding out the truth."

"You need to stop doing this," I complain when her words hit exactly where she intends them to.

"Just think about it, yeah?" she says quickly before there's a crashing at the front door and Dec and Liam both stumble into the room.

CHAPTER THREE

THE SUN'S streaming through the window when I wake. I'm hot, covered in a sheen of sweat, and I'm hard as fucking steel. It doesn't take much brainpower to know whom I was dreaming about. I woke up multiple times last night with the image of her in my head.

Damn Liv for making me talk about her.

Once I've had a very long and cold shower, I make my way down to the kitchen to get coffee. I told Dec I'd be at his surf shack first thing, but seeing as it's almost ten am already, I guess he knows I'm going to be late.

Not needing to get a job has been pretty great. It's meant I've been able to help Dec out when he started his business and with renovating this house when he first bought it, but right now I could really do with a distraction that a career could give me.

When I get to the kitchen, I find Liv sat with a mug in her hands, listening to Liam doing his morning radio show.

"You know you don't have to listen to him every morning, right?"

"Fuck off," she grunts, her cheeks heating with embarrassment from being caught. "How are you feeling?"

Shrugging, I set about filling my mug.

"Did you think about what I said?"

I bite back my initial response because *of course* I fucking thought about what she said. I can't get it—*her*—out of my damn head. I don't get to answer because ringing distracts both of us.

"Are you going to get that?"

Reaching into my pocket, I pull my phone out. I don't need to look at the screen to know who it is. I had two missed calls from Chris after my shower. The fact that he's chosen not to leave voicemails this time has dread knotting my stomach. As much as I might try to ignore what's happening in London, I know that I can't. I also know that Mum and Lauren might not be coping as well as I hope they might be.

Just because I'm glad the fucker's dead, it doesn't mean everyone will feel that way.

"Well?" Liv prompts as I stand staring at it like it's about to explode.

Sucking in a breath, I swipe the screen and bring it to my ear.

"Hello."

"I thought you were ignoring me," is the first thing Chris says, but he doesn't allow me any time to respond before diving straight into the reason for his call. "I need you to do something for me."

"What?" The knot tightens and I find myself leaning forward against the counter, waiting for his next words.

"I need you to go to the office and find me a load of paperwork."

All the air rushes from my lungs. "Can't anyone else do it?" Liv's stare burns into my back but I refuse to turn and look at her.

"Your mum and Lauren have enough going on. Neither of them has been to the office since...and I don't want to make them. I don't want either of them hurting more than they need to be right now." The memories that have been haunting me hit me once again. Image after image of Lauren runs through my mind. My heart starts to race and my hands tremble.

She's not going to want me there, but fuck if I don't need her.

Clenching the fist of my free hand, I try to get myself together.

"Ben, are you still there?"

"Yeah, yeah. I'm here. What is it you need?"

Lowering the phone from my ear, I rest both my palms on the counter and hang my head, trying to catch my breath. I've always hoped this moment would come. That I'd have to go back. That I'd get a chance to reclaim what's rightfully mine. But now the time's here, I'm more terrified than I ever expected to be.

"You're going," Liv states, the sound of her voice dragging me from my panic. Turning my head, I glance over my shoulder at her. Her eyes drill into me, her lips pressed into a hard line. "Whatever it is, the reason you're so scared, you need to get over yourself and be there for Lauren and your mum."

"It's been six years. Six long fucking years since *he* sent me away.

"Fuck, Ben." I wince at her use of my real name, and she doesn't miss it.

"I've had no contact with Mum or Lauren since that day. For all they know, I could be dead. I've no idea what'll happen when I show my face."

She nods as she thinks. "You know you don't have a choice, right? Do you want me to go with you?"

"Thank you, but if I'm doing this, I should do it alone."

Getting up, she walks over and throws her arms around my waist. Dropping my head, I press a kiss to her hair and allow her warmth to ground me.

"You've got this. Your mum needs you right now."

"And what about Lauren?"

Liv blows out a breath. "If she loved you back then, then I'm sure she'll love you even more now. Give yourself some credit—you're a pretty good catch."

A lump forms in my throat and I have to fight the tears that sting my eyes. "Is that right?" I love her positivity, but I have a feeling none of what's to come is going to be that easy.

"Now, stop standing here wasting time with me. Go and get your girl." After unwrapping her arms from me, she gives me a sweet, encouraging smile and pushes me in the direction of the stairs.

I know I should be packing something, but the second I'm in my room, I just stand there. After years of locking everything down, fear of going back floods me. I can't deny there isn't a little excitement mixed in though. I'm desperate to know if they're both okay, to just see them again and take in how much—or how little—has changed over the years.

Instead of reaching for a bag, I pull open the drawer beside my bed and dig out my old phone. I took the SIM out the second I got on the train when I walked away that day. I believed every word of Nick's threats, so I didn't want to be traced. It's why I left my car behind. I could never bring myself to get rid of the phone, though—not when it was full of photos of our short time together.

I'm amazed when it turns on. It's been quite a while since I caved to my need to see her face. I get the usual warning about not being able to connect to a network before I pull up the photos. My heart aches the second I look into her blue eyes. She looks so young and carefree, exactly how she should at eighteen. She only had the slightest inkling of what was going on around her, how much her dad was controlling every single part of her life. I knew she wanted to live in that house almost as much as I did, but also like me, she didn't have a choice. Only it was for a very different reason. I refused to move out because I needed to ensure Mum was safe. She didn't have a choice because her dad was an abusive, controlling wanker.

Eventually, I get my arse in gear and I pack a duffle full of clothes. My entire body vibrates with nervous energy as I leave my room and make my way down the stairs. I've already had my life shattered once, but for some reason I feel like this is the beginning of me having to start over once again. Just this time, it could well be in the place I wanted to be the whole time.

"Call me if you need anything," Liv calls from the front door just as I'm about to climb into my car.

"Thank you." I really mean it. I'm not sure what I'd have done this last few days without her.

I HOPED the journey would give me the time to figure out what I was going to do once I got to London, but as I sit in my car in the street where the Johnson & Son's office is, I'm no closer to knowing.

I've no idea why Chris thought I should do this. I've no idea if I even know anyone who still works here. They might all think I'm some stranger trying to rob the place when I walk inside and start rummaging through Nick's office.

Erica was probably my closest friend in the years

before leaving, but if she's still here, she'll probably hate me just as much as Mum and Lauren for walking away like I did. I'd rather not be on the wrong end of her fiery temper.

Reading through the message Chris sent me earlier that lists everything he needs to get Nick's estate in order, I blow out a steadying breath. I'm not stupid; he could have asked any one of the Johnson & Son's employees to find this shit, but he knows me too well. He knew it would be the push I needed to get my arse up here.

It's now or never.

Throwing the door open, I step out and get my first taste of fresh air since I left Devon hours ago.

As I walk towards the building's entrance, it's like I'm twenty again. I'm suddenly struck with the memory of the night I surprised Lauren when her dad demanded she work late.

I'd had plenty of indecent thoughts about bending her over her dad's desk and fucking the life out of her, but fuck, the real thing was so much more than I ever could have imagined.

That desk should have been mine. It had my name etched into it from the day I was born, but that motherfucker appeared in my life and trampled over everything that was meant to be. If I didn't know that my dad had died of natural causes, I'd truly believe he'd had something to do with it just so he could step into his life and fill his shoes. Not that he'd ever been able to. Dad was a shrewd businessman; he loved this company almost as much as he loved Mum and me. Nick, on the other hand, was nothing but an untrustworthy scumbag. I didn't have the time to figure out what he was doing, but there were definitely dodgy dealings going on.

The hallways are empty and my footsteps echo as I walk along the tiled floor to the office entrance. I try to focus on what I need to do and push the lingering memories from my mind.

My plan is simple: go in, get what I need, and get out. I don't want to cause any drama. Ideally, I'd like to not even be noticed, but I know that's wishful thinking.

Standing in front of the office door, I clench and unclench my fists in an attempt to ease the tension in my body.

I push the door open, look ahead, and march into a space I know like the back of my hand. I basically grew up in this office. From as early as I can remember, I used to come to work with dad. I'd help him with his photocopying, shredding, and licking envelopes when I was a kid. I remember the hours I would spend listening to him and Mum talk about the goings on in the office and I'd soak it all up like a sponge, knowing that one day it was going to be mine. As the years went on, he showed me more and more, and by the time he died when I was fourteen, I already had a pretty good understanding of how the business worked. Knowing that in a few years I'd be able to keep his and my granddad's legacy alive by taking over helped get me through losing both of them in quick succession.

Then *he* swooped in and saved the day.

Or so Mum thought.

She looked at him like he was her knight in shining armour. As far as she could see, he dragged her from the dark pit of grief and depression she'd fallen into, and he'd rescued the business that was on the verge of collapse when she couldn't deal with it alone.

I saw through his façade. None of his actions were to help Mum or me; they were for his own benefit, his own gain. He was one selfish motherfucker.

I was just a kid. There wasn't all that much I could do about the tornado that was my stepdad, but Nick wasn't aware that the company basically ran through my veins. He didn't know that I was watching his every move and noting every questionable decision he made from a distance. I had every intention of bringing him down.

I just didn't get the chance.

As glad as I might be that he's gone, a little disappointment that I didn't get to expose his true colours makes my steps falter. I stumble on the threshold of the office and I immediately feel eyes on me.

When I look up, I find every member of staff staring in my direction with their chins dropped and their eyes so wide that some look on the verge of popping out…none more so than Erica.

CHAPTER FOUR

ERICA'S EYES bore into mine and her features stiffen with anger. Her hurt at my sudden departure all those years ago is clear in her eyes. All my fears about what everyone must think of me come rushing to the forefront. It's not until someone moves at the back of the office that I manage to rip my gaze away from her, but the moment I look over, I find the one person I wasn't expecting. Staring back at me with furious, red-rimmed eyes is Lauren.

My breath catches and my heart twists painfully in my chest as I take in her exhausted face. Every part of me aches to move, to get close to her, to touch her, but even from here I can tell it's the last thing she wants.

"Lauren," I breathe, but there's no way she hears my whisper with the distance between us.

I stand, frozen to the spot, as she drags her bag across the desk. All the paperwork flutters to the floor followed by a loud bang as something more significant falls victim to her hasty escape.

"Lauren," I repeat, managing to find my voice this time.

"Don't." A tiny pair of hands slamming down on my chest makes me look down to the person in front of me. "Don't. You. Fucking. Dare," Erica seethes. She might only be small, but my chest stings by the time she's finished. "You've already done enough damage. You don't get to show up unannounced and throw her world into even more turmoil. She deserves more than that—*more than you.*" Erica's lip curls in disgust. It's my first taste of the kind of mess I left behind when I was forced to leave.

Every set of eyes in the office is still on us. As I glance at each of them, there are a couple I recognise but many that I don't. I almost laugh when I see Betty standing with a mug of tea halfway to her lips. Of course she's still here.

I just about manage a little smile in Betty's direction before Erica's fingers wrap around my wrist and I'm pulled towards the office. For such a small person, she's got some serious strength. The door slams behind us and she turns her wrath back towards me.

"Erica," I sigh. "I just came for some paperwork. I don't need—"

"I don't give a fuck what you need, Ben. What the fuck are you doing here? You've had what...six years to show your fucking face. Were you so scared of him that you had to wait until he was dead to come back?"

"Scared?" I can't help but laugh. "You think I was scared of that motherfucker? Jesus, what bullshit did he spew to you lot?"

"The truth, by the looks of it." Her hand lands on her hips and her eyebrows rise almost to her hairline as she waits for my response.

"I haven't got time for this. I don't owe you anything. There are only two women who need to know the truth, and one of them just stormed out."

"Oh, well that's fucking lovely. I was here, picking up the pieces of the mess you left behind you, and you think you don't owe me anything. You're almost as bad as he was." She nods towards Nick's desk and I see red. How fucking dare she compare me to him.

"Fuck you, Erica. You've no idea what happened

that day. No idea of the threats he made, of the reason I did what I did."

"Try me. We were friends—best friends, if you don't remember. Hit me with it."

"Not now. I just need—"

"Paperwork. You said." Spinning on the spot to collect her thoughts, she pins me with another harsh look. "This is bullshit, Ben. You think you're the only one with issues? You think you're the only one with secrets no one else will understand? Well, you're wrong. We might not know the whole truth about why you suddenly vanished in the middle of the night, but things haven't been all sweetness and fucking light while you've been away. We haven't all been sat around our fucking campfires singing Kumbay-fucking-a. And for your information, your mum and Lauren weren't the only ones who n-needed y-you." Her voice cracks and her lip trembles.

Guilt stronger than I've ever known engulfs me as I watch her body start to shake with emotion. Closing the distance between us, I realise for the first time that me leaving didn't just affect two women, but potentially everyone around me. I don't think I appreciated what I really had here.

I wrap my arms around her shoulders. She tries

to fight to start with, but she soon gives up and allows me to comfort her.

Breathing in her familiar scent, I remember what a good friend she was to me. I'd cast her aside like she meant nothing.

"I'm so sorry. Things back then were... complicated. I did the only thing I could at the time. Nick wasn't..." I trail off, not really wanting to get into this now. "Let me just say that what happened in reality probably wasn't quite how he made it out to be. I didn't leave willingly; I can promise you that."

She nods like she understands and pulls back so she can look at me. "Trust me, I know how he operated better than most. I don't think you'll shock me with anything you tell me, but you should have fought for her. You should have done whatever it took, not just run at the first sign of trouble."

My heart twists and my stomach turns over as I watch her walk out of the office. Resting back on the edge of the desk behind me, I take a few steadying breaths.

I've told myself that same thing time and time again, but nothing will change what happened. At the time, leaving seemed like the best thing for Lauren. I wasn't going to do anything that might make her life worse, and I had no intention of being the one to ruin her relationship with her dad. She wasn't stupid; she knew he wasn't going to win Dad of the Year or anything, but if she knew the truth... I lost my dad way too early, and I'll be fucked if I'm the reason someone else loses theirs. Even if he was a monster.

Despite his arsehole ways, Nick loved Lauren the best way he knew how. If he wasn't such a wanker, I might have been jealous.

But maybe I was wrong. Maybe I should have stood my ground and fought for her. If I'm honest with myself, I knew some of the crap Nick spewed was true. I wasn't good enough for her. I was the bad boy and she was the princess. It never would have ended well. I was her dirty secret. She may have told me that she didn't want to keep what was between us hidden, but it was easy to say that when the outside world didn't know what was going on.

The murmuring of voices from outside the office eventually filters through and I'm reminded of why I'm here. Pushing myself from the desk, I set about rummaging through the filing cabinets until I find what I need.

Just like the moment I first walked in, when I open the door and look out over the office beyond, everyone stops what they're doing and looks up at me. A number of eyes narrow in anger; others just look confused. It's good to know my memory wasn't banished quite as quickly as I was.

Erica appears from the kitchen just as I take a step towards the exit. I've no interest in hanging around here and answering all their bullshit questions. There are only two people who deserve answers, and they're my next stop.

"Ben, wait," she calls, but I don't stop moving.

She runs to catch up with me, but I'm already in the hallway by then.

"Look," she says, placing her hand on my arm and attempting to spin me her way. "I'm sorry, okay?" Those words have me looking back at her. "You've no idea what it was like here after you left, and you turning up like that was just a bit of a shock."

"None of that was by choice, Erica. I had no intention of leaving."

"I...I know. Well, I don't know, but I can only imagine how things went down."

The depth of understanding I see reflected back at me both surprises and scares me in equal measures. But then, I guess she's worked closely with Nick for years. She must have some clue as to what a manipulative bastard he was.

I open my mouth to say something, but I don't get a chance.

"You don't have to explain right now. You've got more important things to deal with. Lauren's waited long enough to find out the truth, don't you think?"

Nodding, I give her a sad smile and walk away.

"We'll catch up soon, yeah? If you need anything, you know where I am." I give her a quick nod, but I'm too intent on getting out of there to respond.

Dumping the folder full of paperwork on my passenger seat, I rest my head back against the headrest. I don't really know how I was expecting that to go, but it certainly wasn't what happened. The image of Lauren's sad eyes and exhausted face fills my mind once again, and my fists clench. Even after death, that motherfucker manages to hurt her.

Erica's right. It's time she learnt the truth. Turning on the ignition, I start a journey that I've made a million times before, except so much is different now. The corner shop I used to buy lunch from is now a hairdresser's, there's a new supermarket, and as I get closer to home, I find that they've managed to somehow shoehorn in a load more houses.

I park in a space a little down the street when I see the main gates to the house are closed.

As a kid, this place was my haven. I loved being here as much as Mum and Dad did and knowing my dad and grandad both designed and built it meant it was even more special. No other kids at school had homes like that. I always hoped it would be mine one day to bring my own family up in, but as I walk up to the front door, none of those old feelings are there. Everything I loved about this place has been tainted by *him*.

After ringing the bell a few times and getting no response, I make my way around the rear of the house. I can't believe my luck when I get to the French doors. This house must be worth well over two million by now, yet no one's bothered to fix the dodgy back door. Exactly like when I was a teenager, if I twist the handle just right, the door slides open. It allowed me to sneak in and out hours past curfew many times over the years.

Mum and Dad were never really that strict. They didn't have to be; I was a good kid. But after Dad died and Mum moved Nick in, things changed. I was a teenager hell bent on ruining my life, and he was a dickhead who couldn't deal with an unruly teenage boy. I had to be in by ten at the latest every night, or he would lock the house down. Mum caught me sneaking in loads of times. She was well aware of the broken door, but it was never fixed.

Sadness runs through me. That could be the exact reason it's still not been fixed. She's holding out hope that one day I might just sneak back in. It was like she was giving me permission to do what I needed to do. She was drowning in grief after my father's death, but she couldn't have been blind enough not to see how Nick came in and basically took over our lives.

The second I step inside, the familiar scent of home fills my nose. Nostalgia hits me so strong that I stumble back against the door. Images of happy times with my parents, my grandparents, and Lauren play out like a movie in my mind. Innocent memories like childhood birthdays, family meals and Christmases; along with ones that have my temperature soaring like taking Lauren on the island after our failed attempt at cake making.

Walking over to the table, I fall down onto a chair and drop my head into my hands. In one sense, that weekend with her still feels like it was yesterday; but being back here now it feels like a lifetime ago. I can still vividly remember how she tasted mixed with icing sugar and cocoa powder.

My cock twitches as I relive that morning with

her. Six years on and just the memory of her alone still affects me like she did back then.

Although there were three cars parked in the driveway, the house is in silence. After it being a loving family home filled with laughter for years, the silence and coldness became normal pretty quickly once Nick moved in. I guess nothing's changed. The place still looks like a show home.

After getting myself a glass of water, I sit back down at the table and pull my phone from my pocket. I find a message from Liv and a smile twitches the corners of my lips.

GOOD LUCK. Call if you need anything x

I JUST START to type a reply when the slam of the front door echoes around the empty house.

A lump jumps into my throat and, as footsteps get closer, my stomach threatens to bring up the water I just drank.

Sucking in a breath, I wait for someone to walk around the corner and into the kitchen to find me.

"Oh my god!" Mum squeals, at first in fright, but

the second she registers it's me, her face softens and her knees buckle.

I'm out of my seat and about to reach for her when someone else steps into the room and beats me to it.

A pair of very cold and angry eyes find mine. My mouth goes dry.

Lauren supports Mum until she's found her strength again. Rushing forward, her petite body slams into mine and she wraps her arms around my waist so tight it's hard to breathe.

"Oh my god, my baby," she sobs into my chest.

Tentatively, I lift my hands and rub them up and down her back as she cries. The whole time, my eyes hold Lauren's. Everything I feared is looking back at me. She hates me. Any hope I might have had that she'd be glad to see me is gone. I've never seen her look so furious, and I've no doubt she's not going to hold back once she gets the chance.

"Lauren," I breathe, desperate to connect with her somehow.

Narrowing her eyes at me once more, she drops them to Mum, who's still attached to me, and then turns and leaves.

The breath I didn't realise I was holding comes rushing out of me. My eyes sting and I struggle to catch my breath again as regret, guilt, hope and love assault me all at once.

I'm frozen to the spot, staring at where she was. It's only movement against my chest that drags me from my living nightmare.

Mum looks up at me through teary, devastated eyes, and a giant lump forms in my throat. Seeing the evidence of what my leaving did to her breaks my heart. I did what I did for them, but looking at her now, I fear I may have made the wrong decision.

CHAPTER FIVE

"I'M SORRY ABOUT YOUR T-SHIRT," Mum says sadly when she pulls away from me and finds the fabric soaked through.

"It's nothing," I mumble, not really knowing what to say. It might have been obvious that she was happy to see me to begin with, but now I can't read her.

Placing her palms on my rough cheeks, she stares deep into my eyes before focusing on every single one of my features.

"There were days I convinced myself that you must have been dead." Hearing her admission makes my insides ache with regret. "I didn't understand any other reason why you'd just disappear like that. This was your home, Ben. You had people who loved you under this roof and you just upped and left in the middle of the night."

"It was complicated, Mum." My voice is deep and rough as I try to contain the emotions running rampant around my body.

She stares at me for a few more minutes before schooling her features and stepping away.

"I don't see how," she snaps. Her eyes darken and suddenly I'm a six-year-old boy who's been caught doing something he shouldn't be. "That girl was head over heels for you, and you disregarded her like she was a piece of shit on your shoe." Her anger seems to come from nowhere, the grieving widow from moments ago long gone.

"You think I did that by choice?" I bellow back. "You really believe this is all my fault? I'm your son. I thought you knew me better than that."

Her face drops. I hate to cause her more pain, but the little faith that she has in me hurts more.

"Did *he* really have you that convinced by his act that you truly think that of me?"

She sucks in a breath, tears filling her eyes. "Have some respect."

"Respect?" I ask with a laugh. "He doesn't deserve it. The man was a scumbag, Mum, and it's about time you acknowledged the truth."

The moment she slides down the wall she's backed up against and breaks down in sobs, I know I've gone too far. She's right. He's just died; I need to be a little more sensitive for her sake. She's already dealing with enough. I didn't come here with the intention of making things harder.

Getting down on my haunches in front of her, I pull her hands away from her face and look at her. I'm reminded of the fact that no matter how much of a monster I knew my stepdad to be, he managed to control everyone else around him to the point that they'd never question him. It never worked on me. It's one of the reasons we were never going to see eye to eye.

"I'm going to have a lie down," Mum whispers, casting her eyes over my shoulder.

Helping her stand, she leans on me enough to show she's not going to make it up the stairs alone. With my arm around her waist, I silently lead her towards the stairs and up to her room.

Her breath catches as we come to a stop beside the bed and her eyes land on two photographs. One of them I haven't seen for a very, very long time.

Sitting on her bedside table is not only a photograph from her and Nick's wedding day, but also one from the day she married my dad.

Dropping down onto the edge of the mattress, she stares at both of them, tears silently dropping from her eyes.

"I don't know what I did wrong. I lost the only three men I've ever loved." It's so quiet, I almost miss it, but knowing I'm one of those three is like a knife to the heart.

"You didn't do anything wrong. I'm not going anywhere, okay?"

She nods, but I don't think she believes a word of it. And why would she?

I leave the room with a heavy heart. She doesn't deserve any of this. It was bad enough she lost her first husband, the love of her life; she shouldn't have to lose another.

Closing the door quietly, I go to head back downstairs, but at the last minute, I continue forward towards *my side* of the house, as it was always known, with two en suite bedrooms. Coming to a stop at my closed bedroom door, I wonder what the inside's going to be like. Did they bin all my stuff? Did they throw me away like I never existed?

I'm just about to open the door to find out when a noise from behind stops me. The closer I get to her bedroom door, the louder the sobs become.

Running my hands over my now shaved hair, I

fight with what I should do. Every inch of my body is screaming to go in and comfort her, but my head knows she won't accept it.

I don't deserve for her to accept it.

After a few seconds, I back away. If there's ever going to be any kind of relationship between us again, I need to allow her to come to me. I've already caused enough pain to last her a lifetime.

Walking back up to my door, I push it open and step inside. What I find shocks the hell out of me.

I was expecting it to be empty or maybe turned into another bland guest bedroom. What I wasn't expecting was to find it exactly the way I left it.

"Fucking hell," I mutter, walking farther into the room and taking in everything I left behind.

It's exactly as I remember. There are still piles of CDs next to the player, as if I'm about to return to play them. The TV remote is sitting on my bedside table where it always was, and my charger is next to it, waiting for my phone. There's even one of my hoodies draped over the chair by the window.

Sitting down on the edge of the bed, I fight to drag in a couple of deep breaths. I expected Nick to have skipped all my stuff the first chance he got.

Seeing my room as it always was has the first tingles of hope trying to nudge their way in. It makes me start to believe that maybe not all that much has changed and that I can fit back into the life I should have here. The place I've always belonged could be my home once again.

Falling back onto my bed, I breathe in the familiar scent. Feelings I hardly remember wash through me. Contentment, safety, true happiness. That's what this house used to be to me, and it can be again. With him gone and no longer controlling everyone's lives, I can finally have what I've always wanted.

I make a plan and stay where I am, enjoying the feeling of my bed beneath me and being surrounded by all my childhood things. That is, until a shiver of awareness runs down my spine.

Propping myself up on my elbows, I look to the door. My heart drops when I don't find who I was expecting—until I see movement of a shadow.

I don't waste any time. Jumping from the bed, I rush to the doorway. I'm desperate for time alone with her.

When I pull the door wide, her eyes fly up to mine in shock. Her mouth drops open, but I beat her to it.

"Lauren," I breathe. I love being able to say her name once again.

Her tired and bloodshot eyes hold mine. I can see fire burning behind them. She probably hopes her anger will scare me off.

Her face softens the longer we stare at each other, and to my surprise, when I reach for her hand and pull her closer, she follows my lead.

I gasp when her breasts gently press against my chest. My heart hammers as all the feelings that I've spent the last six years burying come rushing back.

"Fuck, I've missed you," I admit, staring deep into her light-blue eyes.

They visibly darken the second the words are out of my mouth.

"Fuck you, Ben. Fuck you!" she hisses, backing away and putting her arms up to keep me from coming after her. She bumps back against the wall at the same time as sobs rack her body. "Y-you d-don't get to d-do this," she stutters out through her tears. "You don't get to just turn back up and act like nothing happened. Like you didn't abandon us. Abandon *me*."

She looks at me, her lids lowered and her eyes full of water. There might only be a few feet between us, but it still feels like miles.

My fingers twitch to reach for her and pull her to me. My muscles ache with the need to comfort her.

As I take a step forward, her eyes flash with concern, but I push past it. The moment her warmth presses against my chest, I feel like I can breathe for the first time in years. My arms wrap tightly around her and I hold her as she cries and trembles against me.

I don't think she's aware as I move us from the hallway and into the privacy of my bedroom.

"I'm sorry," she says after many long, incredible minutes in my arms.

I know she doesn't need me to say anything. I bite down on my tongue to stop myself. I lower my eyes—it's the first time I take in what she's wearing.

"Is that your boyfriend's?"

"What?"

"Your hoodie. Is it your boyfriend's?" I know the moment she remembers because her eyes crinkle at the sides. I'm almost convinced I've got to her, but in a split second, they harden, and she jumps from my lap.

"No, Ben. You have no right to ask me those kinds of questions." She goes to leave. I should allow her, but I'm a selfish bastard who's missed her more than I'm willing to admit right now.

"Wait. I've ordered dinner. Is Thai still your favourite?"

Stopping in the doorway, she looks over her shoulder. "Is it from Thai Emerald?"

"Of course. I wouldn't get it from anywhere else."

She narrows her eyes at me, she's trying to look angry, but she knows as well as I do that she'll do anything for their Phat Thai.

"This doesn't mean anything."

Following her down towards the kitchen, I stop briefly to tell Mum I've sorted dinner, but she doesn't respond. I'm desperate to do something to help, but aside from being here, I'm not really sure what else to do for her. I can still vividly remember the depression she fell into after Dad died; I can only hope it's not as bad this time.

The second my foot hits the bottom step, the doorbell rings. I answer it and thank the guy while Lauren crashes around in the kitchen. When I get there, the table is laid with plates and glasses.

"What would you like to drink?" she asks politely, but it's far from her usual kind tone.

"Water would be great, thanks."

"We have beer if you'd like one."

I've used alcohol more times than I can count to help me drown out the reality of my life for the past few years. Now I'm back, with the potential to finally make everything right, it's time I stopped using it as a crutch.

"No, thank you. Water's perfect."

She nods, but she still looks at me curiously. "Well, if you don't mind, my life's shit right now," she says, placing my drink down and filling herself a very large glass of wine and taking a sip.

She sighs as she savours the taste and my eyes drop to the smooth lines of her neck as she swallows. My insides clench and my cock twitches as I imagine dropping my lips to that soft skin.

Her glass slams down on the table and drags me from my fantasies. I watch as she huffs out a frustrated breath before she digs inside the takeout bag for her beloved Phat Thai.

"I'm sorry about your dad, Lauren."

"Are you?" she snaps, her eyes finding mine.

"I'm sorry you've lost a parent. I know how hard that is." I keep any unpleasant words I might want to spew about him to myself. The time will come where I'm going to have to tell her everything, but tonight, I just want us to eat. I want to spend time with her. To just be able to look at her. I want to pretend for an hour or so that things aren't totally fucked up.

"I'm doing okay." Her voice is weak and unconvincing. I can tell by her tired eyes and sad expression that she's anything but okay, but I don't point it out.

We eat in silence, but it's not as awkward as it could be. Just being in her presence brings me a kind of peace I've not experienced in such a long time.

Mum eventually appears, looking worse for wear. She joins us at the table but forgoes the food in favour of the wine. I bite my tongue from chastising her for drinking on an empty stomach. Turning up unannounced following the death of her husband and proceeding to tell her what to do is sure to go down like a lead balloon.

"You two go and relax. I'll clean all this up," I offer, once Lauren and I have finished eating.

Mum immediately gets up, and after thanking me unconvincingly, takes herself and her wine into the living room. Lauren hangs around a little, watching me curiously as I start to tidy up.

"What?"

"N...nothing." Raising my eyebrows, I wait for her to elaborate. "It's just...you're different."

"Different? Is that meant to be a good or bad thing?" My physical changes since the last time she saw me are quite obvious. My annoying teenage floppy hair has been shaved off, and I've spent many, many hours in the gym as I fought to forget and put this place behind me. I'm probably double the size of the boy she remembers.

"That's yet to be determined." Her eyes drop from mine in favour of my body. She bites down on her bottom lip as they take me in. It's clear she's happy with this change at least.

Leaning my hip against the counter, I wait with a smirk playing on my lips while she takes her fill.

She stills the second she realises what's she's doing. When she finds the amusement covering my face, her eyes narrow and her lips press into a thin line. "Don't think about getting any crazy ideas." Stepping up to me, she pokes me in the chest. If it's meant to hurt, she needs to think again.

Wrapping my hand around her delicate one, I pull her against me and put my lips to her ear.

"I'm not getting any ideas, Lauren. I never forgot them."

She gasps and fights to get away from me. I'll allow her to take the space she needs.

For now.

CHAPTER SIX

I HARDLY GET a wink of sleep. Knowing she's just over the corridor is torture. My constant stream of thoughts wondering if she was in her own bed thinking about me and what we once had kept my dick rock-hard all night. It didn't seem to care how many times I came with thoughts of her in my head. The second I allowed my mind to drift once again, up it popped.

I'd like to think I'd become fairly skilled at keeping thoughts of her at bay, focusing on other aspects of my life and trying to distract myself with other women, but one look at her, and just like six years ago in the kitchen, she's the only thing I can see. The only thing I want.

My eyelids are heavy with exhaustion when I

eventually get up the next morning. The house is silent, so even though it's long past what most people would call early, I open the curtains and windows in the hope of brightening the place up a little, then kick-start the coffee machine. It's not the one I remember, so it takes me a few minutes to figure out how it works, but soon the scent of the beans fills the room and I already start to feel a little more alert.

With my steaming mug in hand, I slide open the doors that cover the entire back wall of the house and step out into the morning sun. It's not quite the fresh sea air that I've become used to, but it's not city smog either.

Falling down onto the swing seat, I rest my head back and try to enjoy the peace and quiet. It doesn't work; my mind still runs at a mile a minute with images of Lauren. I'm desperate to take her pain away, to make all of this better for her. But I know that's not possible.

Holding her to me last night felt so incredible, but I'm not stupid enough to think she's going to allow that to happen again anytime soon. She's had years to build up her walls when it comes to me, and I'm going to have one hell of a fight on my hands to knock them down.

She thinks I betrayed the one promise I made to

her by leaving. I told her I'd always protect her, and that was exactly what I was doing. Protecting her from the knowledge of who her dad really was. Protecting their relationship. That was the most important thing to me at the time.

"Why are you here, Ben?" The sound of her soft, sweet voice has my heart pounding and picks my head up from where it was resting. I didn't hear her join me, but when I look over, she's stood in the doorway staring down the garden.

I allow myself a moment to take her in. Her blonde hair is in a mess and piled on top of her head. Her face is fresh and clear of make-up, although when she turns I know I'll see pain and sadness in her eyes. She's wearing that damn man's hoodie she had on last night and what I assume is a tiny pair of pyjama shorts just poking out the bottom, leaving her mile-long, tanned legs on full display.

Shifting to a slightly more comfortable position, I clear my throat and try to remember what her question was.

She must get bored of waiting, because after a few seconds, she turns her stare on me, her hands coming up to rest on her hips. Her attempt at attitude makes me want to laugh, but the hardness of her features stops me.

Widening her eyes, she continues to impatiently wait while I battle with what to say.

None of my answers are going to go down very well.

"I..."

"You were brave enough to show your face now Dad's gone?"

I open my mouth to argue, but in a way what she's saying is correct.

"No, Lauren. It's more complicated than that."

"Is it? Because the way I see it..." She walks closer, but her angry eyes never leave me. "You got scared, you ran, and you continued running until you no longer had to. The risk of coming home has gone, and you are free to do whatever your selfish, pig-headed self wanted to do. You should just do us all a favour and crawl back to wherever it was you ran to."

When she runs out of steam, she's right in front of me, staring hate-filled daggers down at me.

Slowly standing, my eyes run up the front of her until I find hers. They're dark and angry, but I also see more in them. Our bodies are only a breath apart, and her heat seeps into me. I clench my fists to stop me reaching out and pulling her to me.

Her breath tickles over my face as her chest heaves with anger.

"Nothing's changed, has it?" I ask, searching her face and dropping my eyes to her full lips.

"Y-yes. Everything's changed. Everything has changed." Slamming her palms against my chest, I fall back onto the chair as she spins and storms away.

My lips twitch up into a smile. I've gotten to her. She might think her act is fooling me, but I see her. I can see underneath the façade she's trying to show the world.

"SON, it's so good to see you," Uncle Chris says, pulling his front door open later that day.

"You too," I grunt when I find myself dragged into a brief man hug.

"Thank you," he says taking the folder from my hands. "Did you manage to get everything?"

"I think so. All the bank details should be in there. I can always go back if need be. Is everything… as it should be?"

Chris knows I had concerns about Nick's business decisions, but like me, he never found any evidence of any wrongdoing. As our family solicitor for as long as I can remember, Chris has always known the ins and outs of the business, and he's always been in the best position to know if there was anything questionable happening. The fact that he never found anything makes me doubt myself.

"So far so good. We're yet to get the will, but I'm assuming your mum is to get everything. But someone's going to need to take over, and soon." He pins me with a look, and I don't need to ask what he means by that statement.

I always thought the business was my future; but standing here now with it once again in reach, I'm not sure it's what I really want. As much as I've wanted to be back here, I can't deny I'm missing my new life just a little bit.

"How are your mum and Lauren doing?" he asks, changing the subject when I keep my lips sealed.

"Mum's...lost." She didn't show her face this morning. The only reason I knew she was still in her room was the sounds of her cries as I got ready to come here. I knocked, tried to convince her to come down for food, but she ignored me. "And Lauren's...angry."

"You sound surprised."

"Not really. I expected it."

"You need to tell her the truth, you know."

"I will. I just want her to get the funeral done first. I think it's important that she says goodbye to him as she knew him."

"You've got a wise head on those shoulders, boy. Your dad would be proud of you."

The mention of my dad, as always, has a lump climbing up my throat.

Chris looks over when I don't respond, his face full of sympathy. "You know the only person he'd want to take over now is you, don't you?"

Nodding, I sip at the coffee he placed in front of me.

Am I ready for this?

"Are you planning on attending the funeral?"

Looking up over the rim of the mug, I consider his question. I've no intention of going to celebrate that arsehole's life, but it's not about me.

"I think you should, Ben," Chris says, interrupting my thoughts. "Your mum needs all the support she can get right now. God knows it's the only reason I'm going." Seeing the determination on his face warms my heart. I've always felt a little comfort in the fact that Mum had Chris here looking out for her; but seeing how important she is to him confirms that I was right in reaching out to him when I left. Chris was Dad's old school friend, but he and Mum have always been quite close. When they both lost their other halves too early in their lives, it only cemented their friendship.

I stay with Chris until I know the office will be empty, then I head straight there. I've always felt close to Dad in the place he spent so much time, building the business, creating his empire, and I need that kind of comfort right now.

I upheaved my life six years ago. Totally started over. Do I want to do that again? The little voice in my head screams that I'm not starting over—I'm coming home. The hesitation I feel about the whole thing doesn't seem to agree with that though.

I spend hours on the phone to the IT support desk as I attempt to log onto the system and see what kind of state everything's in. I have full confidence in the office staff—the ones I know, anyway. It's the late boss who has me desperate to dig around in the background of the business.

I eventually manage to get access, and by the time I look up from emails, quotes, and invoices, it's already dark out.

IT'S WELL gone midnight when I pull up outside Mum's house, so I'm not surprised to find it in darkness. It feels weird not driving my old BMW, but I'm guessing that's long gone after my disappearance. It's certainly not sitting here, waiting for my return.

Flashing from the living room catches my attention the second I open the front door. When I get to the doorway, I find the telly playing to itself and Lauren fast asleep on the sofa.

Switching it off, I crouch down in front of her. "Lauren, you need to go to bed," I whisper.

Her eyelashes flicker, but she's doesn't show any other sign of waking. Reaching forward, I place my hand on her shoulder. She's freezing.

Without thinking, I slide my arms under her body and pull her up against me. She immediately nuzzles into the warmth of my shoulder.

I don't move for a few seconds as I allow myself to enjoy the moment. Dropping my nose to her hair, I breathe her in. My heart races at just being able to hold her again.

"Ben," she whispers. My entire body aches with my need for her.

My arms start to burn by the time I get us up to her room. Kicking the door open, it immediately hits me that although my room was like a time warp when I walked in, hers is very different. Gone are all the girly things she used to try to make the place look like home when she first moved in, and in their place are generic ornaments and fake flowers. It almost looks like a guest bedroom, and it saddens me that part of our past has vanished.

Regretfully, I lower her to her bed. I'm desperate to crawl onto it with her, but I can't imagine that would go down too well when she wakes.

I'm just standing up when her eyes flutter open. The pain she's in makes the light-blue I'm used to so much darker.

"Ben?" My name is a whisper on her lips like she doesn't believe I'm really here. Tingles shoot up my arm when her fingers brush against mine. "Please."

Looking back at her open bedroom door, I hesitate. I want more than anything to crawl into bed with her, but I'm fairly positive that she'll regret it.

"Lauren...I..."

"Just lie with me. I don't want to be alone right now." The hollowness of her voice has my body moving before I've even thought about it. Not that I would ever deny her what she needs.

Toeing my shoes off, I pull my hoodie over my head and drop it to her floor, waiting for her to change her mind. When she doesn't say any more, I climb onto the bed and lie down beside her.

We're not touching, but the heat from her body burns into mine. Fisting the sheet beneath me, I fight not to roll over, not to touch her.

Tension crackles between us. The only sound surrounding us is our heavy breathing. It's the only clue I have that she's as affected by our closeness as I am.

I suck in a sharp breath and my muscles tense when she moves, her arm sliding across my stomach and wrapping around my body. She presses herself against me and holds tight.

"Make it stop. Please, just make it all stop."

"I'm so sorry, baby." She stills the second the last word falls from my lips, and I worry she's going to pull away. But after a moment or two, she relaxes again, and I wrap my arms around her. Silent sobs shake her body, her tears soaking my shirt.

I wish I could take it all away. I remember all too well the pain of losing my dad. Sadly, the only way I know how to make her forget is something she'll probably regret in the morning.

I must eventually fall asleep, because when I pull my eyes open the next morning, I'm alone in Lauren's room. Sitting up, I look around, hoping she'll still be here. I almost smile when the handle of the door on her en suite moves—that is, until I get a look at her. She looks incredible wrapped in a fitted black dress, and her new womanly curves make my mouth water, but the moment I get to her eyes, all my thoughts are forgotten.

"Fuck, Lauren." I rush to get off the bed and she bursts into tears.

"No," she demands the second I'm in front of her. I'm desperate to comfort her, to give her anything to make her feel just that little bit better, but she wraps her arms around herself and turns her face away, cutting me off. "You need to leave. Last night was..."

"Don't do this," I all but beg, reaching up to cup her cheek.

"No, Ben. It was a mistake. All of this is a mistake. You need to leave." She doesn't look at me as she pushes me towards her bedroom door. "Get out. Please, just get out."

The second I step foot in the hallway, her bedroom door slams behind me.

Her cries sound out around me as she falls back against the door. It breaks my heart that she won't allow me to support her through this, although I guess it's no less than I deserve.

Falling down onto the edge of my bed, I try to decide what to do. I really have no desire to go and listen to what an incredible man my stepdad was. How he was a doting husband and father and all the other bullshit I'm sure people will spew. He was nothing but a controlling arsehole, but I guess that's not really the kind of thing you can say at someone's funeral.

I know Chris was probably right yesterday when he said we need to be there for Mum and Lauren, but I'm not really sure what good I'll do.

In the end, it's the thought of the two of them dealing with this alone that has me rummaging through the small bag I brought with me for something suitable to wear to this damn thing.

CHAPTER SEVEN

EVERYONE'S already in the crematorium when I arrive, so it's easy to slip in at the back unnoticed. The room's packed; I can't help but wonder who everyone is. Other than immediate family, I never knew Nick had any real friends, and I can't imagine any of the women he used to spend time with would show up.

I find Mum, Lauren, and Chris in the front row with a couple of others I recognise, and I spot Erica and some work colleagues a few rows back. Guilt hits me that I haven't found time to see Erica since our first meeting the other day. Hopefully, once today is over, we'll be able to catch up properly and she'll be able to help me shed some light on what might or might not be going on with the business.

Hiding in the shadows, the music starts as a small commotion at the entrance causes people to look around. Moments later, a man walks in. Marching past the rows of seats, he makes a beeline for the front. Looking forward, my heart sinks when I find Lauren looking back at him as if she was waiting with a sad smile on her lips.

I can't take my eyes away from them as he steps up to her, pulls her into his arms and kisses the top of her head. He whispers something to her before resting his lips against her head and comforting her.

Fuck. That should be me.

Rubbing my hands over my face, I try to keep my stomach from turning over at the thought of some other guy touching her.

When they eventually part, he pulls her into his side and they take their places in the front row.

I fight the urge to walk out. I didn't want to be here in the first place, but now I've also got to watch as another man comforts the woman who should be mine.

They stay huddled together as he whispers in her ear. My fists clench as my imagination runs wild about what he could be saying.

Her demands that I leave her room this morning suddenly make more sense. I thought she just didn't want me there, but in reality, she spent the night in a bed with a man who's not her boyfriend.

My stomach clenches, and I suck in deep breaths to try to settle it. Thankfully, the vicar stands and starts the ceremony. It might be the last thing I want to listen to, but it's a welcome distraction from the man currently holding Lauren in his arms. I knew coming here was a bad fucking idea.

SENSING that the service is about to come to an end, I slip out of the side door. There's no way I'm giving that motherfucker any more of my time. It's bad enough he got that much—although he's probably up there laughing that I had to watch another man with Lauren the entire time. The image of him holding her while she cried is burned into my mind.

That should have been me.

I should be the one comforting and supporting her. Me. That motherfucker took that away from me the day he made me leave. He allowed an opening for another man to step in and sweep her off her feet.

But instead, I'm in my car, racing towards the one place I know I'll get some solace. Although it'll still be filled with memories of her. I can't seem to go anywhere in this city without reminders of our short time together.

Pulling up into the deserted car park, I turn off the engine and rest my head back. I don't shut my eyes for fear of seeing them again. Instead, I just stare up to the blue, cloudless sky above. It's too good a day for that arsehole. It should be dark and miserable to match his heart.

Fire continues to burn through my veins, and the muscle in my neck pulses with my need to release some tension.

My phone vibrating in my pocket drags me from my depressing thoughts. I intend on ignoring it, but when I see Liv's name looking back at me, I find myself swiping to answer.

"Hey." My voice comes out sounding weak and pathetic even to my own ears.

"Well, that pretty much answers my question about how you're doing." Blowing out a breath, I try to come up with something to say. Thankfully, Liv fills the silence. "It was the funeral this morning, right? Did you go?"

"She's got a boyfriend," is the answer that falls from my lips.

"Oh."

"I should have expected it, but when I found out

she was still living at home, I just assumed..."

"I'm so sorry, Ben."

"I should just come back and get on with my life."

"Is that what you really want?" My response is a sigh, but it's all she needs to hear. "No, I didn't think so. As much as I hate to say it, that's your home, Ben. Your mum, the business...Lauren..."

"Lauren's not mine anymore."

"It doesn't mean she won't ever be. Not everything you want in life falls into your lap. Sometimes, you have to put a little work in. It's time to fight for what you want. For what you deserve."

Liv's words stay with me long after she ends the call. I'm once again left wondering if this is where I'm meant to be.

I avoid the wake. I've no patience for shitty small talk about a man I hated. Instead, I stop at a shop, pick up some beer and spend what's left of the day in the bastard's home office, trying to dig my way through the backlog of emails sitting in his Inbox.

When the front door opens, it's with Chris and Lauren attempting to carry my drunk mother into the house.

"She overdid it a little," Chris says, not that her state really needs any explanation.

"I've got her." Taking over from Lauren, I help Chris get her up to bed.

"She's really not handling this well. I'm worried about her," he says, turning to me once we've shut her bedroom door. "I'm so glad you're here to keep an eye on her."

"I'll do whatever I can." I immediately regret the thoughts I had earlier about heading back to Devon. How could I even consider it when Mum's falling apart?

I say goodbye to Chris, agreeing that he'll come back in a few days with paperwork and Nick's will, so everything can be sorted. I bite my tongue to stop myself demanding he gets everything together faster so we can put that dickhead behind us for good.

A little of the fire from earlier flows through me when I find Lauren staring out the sliding doors at the garden. She's still wearing the dress from the funeral and it hugs her curves and arse perfectly. My old desire burns through me, mixing with my anger and jealousy. It's a dangerous combination.

"How are you doing?" I ask, although I immediately feel stupid for it when Lauren turns her dark eyes on me.

They're cold. Her pain hits me. I'd give anything to take it away right now.

"Fucking peachy," she snaps. I watch from the doorway as she wrenches the fridge door open with more strength than I gave her credit for and pulls out a bottle of wine. I flinch when she slams it down on the marble counter and sets about finding a glass. I almost stop her and tell her to sit down, but if she's anything like me, then I know she needs the distraction of doing something right now.

I wait her out. She knows I'm watching her every move, because every few seconds her hard eyes flick over to me. After drinking half a glass, she turns her glare on me. "What?"

"I'm worried about you."

"Well, isn't that fucking good of you?"

"I...I never stopped caring about you."

"I don't care, Ben. All of...*that*...is in the past. You made your choice, and I was forced to deal with it."

Seeing the pain that I caused her staring back at me is too much. "What else is there to drink?"

Not being able to deal with the images of our time together on repeat in my head, I find myself a bottle of Nick's old vintage whiskey and pour myself a generous measure.

"To everything we lost." If she thinks for one second I mean her father, then she's very, very wrong. The only thing I lost in all of this is her.

She raises her glass and then places it to her lips. My own drink burns my throat, but it never distracts me from her. I take in every movement as she sips at the golden liquid and swallows, followed by her tongue sneaking out to lick her bottom lip.

Fire fills my veins and my cock swells. I need to stop the images in my head. Those from the past are mixing with the one from earlier with her in another man's arms. There's only one way I know for that to happen.

Her eyes darken further, but I fear it's with different emotions to those I'm feeling.

"What are you doing?" she asks in panic when I take a step towards her. Her body visibly tenses, anger vibrating off her.

"You lied to me." I run my eyes all over her face for any more signs that I'm right. Her lids lower, her cheeks heat and her lips part with her increased breathing. "All of that," I say, repeating her earlier words, "is far from in the past. This. Me and you. It'll never be in the past, and you know it just as well as I do."

I'm right in front of her, my hands resting on the cold counter at her back as I cage her against it. Her increased breaths mean her chest is heaving and her breasts are a whisper away from brushing against me.

Dropping my head lower, excitement explodes within me as I watch her eyes drop to my lips. But I don't give her what she wants. Instead, I move to her ear. "Nothing's changed. I can still see desire in your eyes. I can still read your body like it belongs to me. Let me take it away. Allow you to forget."

A needy whimper falls from her lips. I go to move back, but her hands fist my shirt, stopping me from going too far.

Her breath caresses my face as she stares into my eyes. I can practically smell her need for me. Moving forward as if I'm going to make the first move, I brush my cheek against hers. She sucks in a breath as my scruff scratches her soft skin. "Be careful what you wish for, baby. You might not be able to handle the man I've become."

A laugh falls from my lips when her tiny fists slam down on my solid chest.

"You arsehole. You think you can just turn up after all these years and that I'm going to fall at your fucking feet. You're fucking delusional." I allow her some space and take a step back. My eyes drop from hers and run over every one of her tempting curves.

"I can fuck you better than he can any day, and you know it." The corner of my lip curls up in a smirk as she growls and flies at me.

I always enjoyed riling her up, but this is different. Our time apart means the tension between us is explosive.

She punches and slaps wherever she can make contact, but it's only a few seconds before I capture her wrists and pin them both behind her back.

Her harsh breaths rush over my face as she stares at me like she wants to kill me.

"You know I'm right, ba—"

Reaching up on her tiptoes, her lips press against mine, cutting off my words. My fingers release her arms and I crush her body against me. Her lips part the moment I run my tongue along them, and I'm hungrily welcomed inside. Her taste explodes in my mouth. It's just as I remember.

Glass smashes at our feet as we collide with the island, sending our drinks crashing to the floor.

There's no style or finesse to our kiss. It's wet, dirty, teeth clashing and lip biting as we reconnect. My hands explore her new curves—they feel incredible. We still line up like we were made for each other. Her nails scratch at any bit of skin she can find as we fumble our way towards the door.

Grabbing onto her arse, I lift her from the floor. Her legs wrap around my waist and I begin walking us towards the stairs.

Ripping my lips from hers when my lungs burn for air, I focus on not falling with her in my arms.

She has other thoughts though, because no sooner have we broken apart than her lips are on my neck. She kisses and licks up to my ear. I lose my footing as she sucks hard on the sensitive skin, and together we tumble onto the stairs.

"Fuck," I grunt, trying to keep my weight off her.

Giggling, her hands run over my head and I'm pulled down to her lips.

Hitching her leg up around my hip, I grind myself against her. She moans into my mouth and arches her back against the stairs in her need for more.

Her hands find the bottom of my t-shirt and, with my help, she pulls it from my body. Her dainty hands run down my back as I hungrily take her lips once again.

Lifting her, I slip my hands around her back and find the zip of her dress. In seconds it's undone and I'm peeling the fabric from her shoulders. My lips skate down her neck and onto her chest.

I slip the lace covering her breast down at the same time she reaches for my waistband. Sucking her nipple into my mouth, I groan as her tiny hand slides into my boxers and she grips my length.

Not able to wait, I push my jeans and boxers down over my arse and pull her knickers aside, exposing exactly what I want.

Rubbing the head of my cock through her folds, she arches once again, trying to find more of what I have to offer.

I don't give her the chance to ask for it. The second I find her entrance, I slide into her heat. Her walls ripple around me and I swallow down the roar that threatens to tear from my lips.

Gripping onto her hips, my fingers dig in, leaving me no doubt that she'll have a nice reminder of this moment in the morning when she looks down.

I thrust up into her, and she cries out in pleasure, the first signs of her orgasm already showing.

Lifting her arse a little, I find the perfect position to get her off, my memory of what she likes front and centre of my mind. She cries out once again before she falls over the edge. The tightness of her muscles squeezing my cock has me falling with her and I release everything I have inside her.

"Bedroom," she breathes without even opening her eyes.

I'm still inside her as we crash against the wall at the top of the stairs and eventually make it to her bedroom door and tumble inside.

Dropping her to her bed, I make quick work of removing the clothing that's still on my body. If she thinks a quick, angry fuck is it for us, then she's got another think coming.

She's still laid out when I step up to her and pull her dress from around her waist. It's quickly followed by her underwear until there's nothing between us. Climbing on top of her, my hands land on her cheeks and I stare into her eyes as I try to convince myself that this is real. Our breaths mingle and our chests heave. Eventually, my need for her has me dropping my lips to hers. I trail my lips down her jaw and drop them to her breasts, continuing what we started on the stairs.

She whimpers above me and chants my name as I suck one and then the other into my mouth.

"Ben. Please," she begs.

Unable to deny her anything, I slide my hand down her body and circle her clit.

"Fucking hell," I mutter, finding her soaked with the evidence of our previous encounter.

She sucks in a breath when my finger teases her entrance. Her entire body trembles with her desperation for release. Hunger and want fills me with my desire to be the one to give her what she needs.

Finding her entrance, I push one and then two fingers inside her while still licking at her breast. Her breathing increases and her moans get louder.

Just before she's about to fall over the edge, I remove all contact.

Climbing down the bed, I force her thighs apart and stare at her.

She props herself up on her elbows and looks down her body at me. The sight alone almost makes the last six years worth it.

I already knew that I never stopped loving her, but in this moment, with my heart pounding in my chest, I'm surer than ever that she's the only one for me.

I open my mouth to say something, but obviously sensing it's going to be something she can't handle, she softly shakes her head.

Trying to put everything I need to say to her to the back of my mind, I focus on the task in hand.

With my hands on her thighs, keeping her legs wide, I lower my head and circle my tongue around her clit.

She moans when I start to add more pressure—I'm desperate to hear the noise she makes when I tip her over the edge.

The fact that we're not alone in the house is far

from my mind as I slide two fingers inside her and find the place that will ensure an earth-shattering release.

"Oh god, oh god," she chants as I feel the beginnings of her orgasm.

Upping my efforts, I press my tongue harder against her until her entire body tenses under me.

My name is a cry on her lips as her body shatters into a million pieces. I continue stroking her, ensuring it lasts as long as possible. If she remembers one thing tomorrow about this day, then I want to make damn sure it's this.

Her eyes are dazed and glassy when I climb on top of her. Wasting no time, I shift her up higher and slam my lips down on hers. She moans the second her tongue slides against mine, and I know it's because she can taste herself on me.

With one hand holding the back of her head, the other explores her body. I tease her breast and nipple before finding her pussy once again. She's writhing against my fingers almost immediately.

She's been waiting for this moment for six years, just like I have. There's so much I want to say to her right now, but I keep the words inside, scared that one wrong move might be the end. I'm nowhere near ready to walk away from this, but I know it's going to happen. I just need to make the most of the time I have.

She might be fully on-board with this right now, but I've no doubt she's going to regret it. If I was less of an arsehole, I might stop, but I'm fucking powerless to walk away from this woman.

"I need you." I don't need to hear any more. In one move, I'm lined up at her entrance and gently pressing inside.

"Look at me," I demand, pulling back from her lips. She does as I say, and her eyelids flicker open until I'm staring down into her eyes, into her soul. "Me and you," I whisper as I thrust. "Always."

Everything falls into place the moment I'm inside her once again. This is where I'm meant to be. Where I belong.

"What's wrong?" Looking into her concerned eyes, I realise that I've stopped moving.

I can see that warning on her face once again, so I swallow down my words and resume what I started. I thrust into her, and her back arches from the bed and her eyes close.

Dropping my head to her neck, I set about making her scream once again.

CHAPTER EIGHT

I ROLL us over so she's on top. With my hands on her hips, I help her move as she brings us both closer to our releases.

"Lauren," I grunt. I'm so close, but I need her to come first. I need to feel her squeezing my cock tight. "Let me feel you."

She moves her hands from where she was playing with her tits and runs one down her stomach. I watch its descent, desperate to see her bring herself to orgasm.

Her mouth drops open when she finds her clit and I feel the first signs of her impending release.

"That's it. Let go, Lauren." She throws her head back and screams at my demand as she clamps down on me so hard that it forces me into my own release.

I groan as I empty everything I have inside her. Six years of waiting, of imagining I'd get the chance again has a lump growing in my throat and tears stinging my eyes. I feel like a pussy, but I can't help it. I've never felt anything with the other women, and now I'm here, everything is starting to bubble over.

Looking forward, Lauren gazes down at me. Her emotions are clear as day on her face. Thankfully, it isn't regret that is staring back at me. The sadness over what today held is too strong to allow anything else in.

Running my hands around her back, I encourage her to lie down on my chest.

The second our skin connects her body starts trembling. I've no idea what to do to help, other than just hold her.

We stay locked in our embrace for the longest time. The after-effects of my orgasm have long since faded, but having her naked body pressed up against mine ensures my arousal isn't too far away.

I start to think she's fallen asleep and wonder what I should do for the best when I feel her start to kiss the tattoo on my neck. Her lips move over the ink and goosebumps race across my skin.

"It says regret," I whisper, feeling the need to

explain just a small part of the tattoo that wasn't there before.

She sucks in a breath and stills. I panic that I've said the wrong thing, that I've fucked up, but after a second, her fingertip tickles across the ink on my pec.

"You always said you'd get more. They're incredible."

I know the moment she finds it. She stops and every muscle in her body tenses as she sits up and stares down at me.

"Lauren?"

"W-why...why is that there?" She doesn't take her eyes away from the place where her name is inked onto my skin.

"I told you, I never forgot anything about you. Nothing's ever changed for me." Reaching out, I tuck a strand of hair behind her ear, and the gentle touch has her eyes finding mine.

"But—"

Placing my fingers over her lips, I whisper, "Not now. Not tonight."

Rolling her over, I go into her en suite to find a cloth to clean her up with.

My heart jumps into my throat when I return and find her still naked on the bed. Everything I'm desperate to say to her is on the tip of my tongue, but I know she'll never accept it. Not right now, anyway.

Climbing back on to the bed, I encourage her to open her legs and gently clean her up with the warm cloth.

"I didn't use—"

"I'm on the pill," she whispers, regret starting to creep into her tone.

I nod, not really giving a fuck if she wasn't. She's mine, and I'm going to make sure she damn well knows it.

Getting the sense she's about to send me away, I drop the cloth, pull her into my arms and press my lips to hers. I'm not ready to let her go yet.

OUR EXHAUSTION eventually drags us under because, before I know it, I'm opening my eyes to find the room full of sunlight.

Reaching out, I hope to find Lauren sleeping beside me. I need her soft skin pressed up against mine again to remind me that last night wasn't just one incredible dream. Finding the side of the bed next to me empty, my heart drops.

"You need to leave." Déjà vu hits me.

"You need to stop this, Lauren."

"Me?" she asks as if she wasn't a willing participant last night.

"You're the one who keeps inviting me here."

"I don't think I ever—" I raise an eyebrow at her, and she trails off. She knows as well as I do that she wanted it last night. The blush on her cheeks isn't the only evidence.

Throwing the covers off, I shift to the edge of the bed and then stand. Her eyes drop from my face to feast on my body. Hours in the gym as well as surfing means it's a little different to what she was used to. Her chin drops and her tongue licks across her bottom lip. She can try to pretend all she likes that she's not interested anymore, but her body tells a different story.

After a few seconds, she realises what she's doing. "Jesus, Ben. Put it away." Putting her hand up to cover my junk, she casts her eye to the corner of the room.

"You weren't complaining last night." I take a step towards her and push her outstretched arm away. She takes one back, bumping against the door frame.

She swallows and her features harden. "Last night shouldn't have happened."

"But—"

"No buts, Ben. It shouldn't have happened. Our time together ended the moment you walked out. I'm over it...I've moved on."

Her words are the reminder I need. She's taken, yet she spent the night with me. My teeth grind and my fists clench at the thought of her being with someone else.

The cactus sitting on the sideboard beside her catches my eye and I take a few seconds to look around the room I no longer recognise because it looks like a guest room, not one that someone lives in.

When I find her eyes, she knows I've figured it out.

"No," I shout. "No, Lauren. This is bullshit."

"This *bullshit* is my life."

"Why the hell are you here if you don't live here?"

"To look after your mum. Someone had to do it, seeing as she was convinced her only child was dead."

Lifting my hands to my head, I take a step away and try to collect my thoughts. As true as her statement is, it seriously hurts.

"This isn't how it's meant to be, Lauren."

"You don't need to tell me that. I didn't choose

any of this. I was happy. I knew exactly what I wanted and you...you shattered it."

"You think I chose this? You think I walked away without a second thought?"

"Well, didn't you?"

"No, Lauren. I never once chose to walk away from you. The only thing I wanted was you. The only thing I still want is you. I- I—"

"No. You can't do this. It's too late...*it's too late*," she repeats as she side-steps me and storms from the room.

I stare at the closed door she leaves behind her for the longest time. Last night, when she was in my arms, everything felt right again for the first time since I walked away from this house. I knew it wasn't going to last forever, but this right now hurts more than I was expecting it to. How I still feel about her was about to fall from my lips, and she walked away. I guess it's what I deserve, karma or some shit, but fuck if the ache in my chest isn't worse than it's ever been right now.

As much as I want to spend the rest of the day in what was her bed, where so many of my memories are, I collect up my clothes and head towards my own room.

I'm just closing her door when someone in the

hallway makes me look up. I find Mum at the top of the stairs, staring at me. I'm grateful I went to the effort of putting my boxers on before leaving the room.

"Do you think that was the best idea?"

The last thing I need right now is having her questioning me and making me feel like a kid again. I haven't had to answer to anyone but myself for years, and I'm not intending to start now.

"Fuck knows, but it's happened now, hasn't it?"

Her chin drops at my harsh tone, and I make my escape. I'm thankful that she looked better than she did yesterday, but selfishly, she isn't my main priority right now.

HANGING around the house all day feeling sorry for myself isn't an option.

Once I'm showered and dressed, I make sure Mum's okay and apologise for snapping at her this morning before heading towards the office. There's plenty to do to keep me distracted.

I wasn't really expecting Lauren to be here, but I'm kind of relieved when I see that I'm right. She obviously needs time to get her head together after what happened. I might not feel guilty about us spending the night together, but I'm sure as shit that she does.

The moment I walk in, Erica is up from her chair and heading my way. She has a weird look on her face as she approaches. She shocks the shit out of me when she doesn't stop at a reasonable distance and instead slams into me and throws her arms around my waist.

I return the gesture and carefully guide her into the office, away from prying eyes.

"Erica, are you—"

I don't get to finish my question because she pulls away from me and looks up. "I'm sorry for going off on you like that the other day. It wasn't fair for me to blame everything on you. It's just...I missed you." She whispers the last bit, her cheeks heating with embarrassment.

"Aw, you missed me?" She laughs as I ruffle her hair like a little kid, but a strange tension continues to radiate from her. Falling down into the office chair behind the desk, I watch as she wrings her hands in front of her and shifts from foot to foot. "What's wrong?"

Her eyes find mine and I swallow when I sense the seriousness of whatever she's about to say.

"You slept with Lauren. What were you

thinking?" My eyes widen. I was not expecting those words to fall from her lips. "If it was that she'd have one roll around in the sack with you and forget all about what happened, then you'll be bitterly disappointed, Ben."

"I know, it's just...I saw her with *him* yesterday and..."

"And?"

"I just couldn't fucking stand the thought of his hands on what's mine."

"She's not yours. She hasn't been for a long time. You gave that up the minute you walked away. Joe's been there for her when she needed someone the most. He's a good guy."

Guilt finally starts to niggle at me. I've no doubt that he's a good guy. If Lauren thinks he's good enough for her, then he probably is. "Is that meant to make me feel any better?"

"No. I'm just telling you how it is. She's been living with him for a while now. I haven't seen her so happy for a long time."

"This isn't helping."

She shrugs and watches as I power up the computer. "So what's the plan?"

"With Lauren? Fuck knows."

"No, I meant for this place."

"Business as usual, I guess. It shouldn't take me too long to get back into it, especially when I've got seasoned pros around like you, of course." The more I say, the paler Erica's face gets. "Now what?"

"How much do you know about the state of the business?"

"Not much, but there's more staff on the payroll than I ever knew and looking at some of the jobs running and the profit margins, things appear to be good...but I'm sensing that might not be the case?"

Erica looks like she's about to throw up. Dread fills my stomach for what's about to come. "Yeah, that's how it looks."

"Go on..."

She lets out a breath, then looks behind her to make sure the door's shut. "I don't think I need to spell out to you what kind of man Nick was." When I don't respond she lowers her voice and continues. "The business is in real trouble, Ben. There's no money."

"But—"

"I know. I know exactly how it looks, because he made me make it look that way."

The ball of dread explodes and my heart starts to race at the thought of him ruining part of my heritage. "You need to start explaining, Erica."

"He started investing the profits. It was fine to start with, but then a few went wrong. He borrowed some money to keep up with wages, but everything spiralled to the point that he couldn't cover it up anymore. So I questioned him when he started demanding that I fudge the numbers."

"I bet that went down well," I mutter, knowing all too well how much he hated to be questioned, even when he was in the wrong.

"I was in a rough place at the time. He knew it and used it to his advantage." Erica doesn't look at me as she says this and my stomach twists.

"Erica?" She falls down into the chair in front of me and drops her head into her hands. "Erica, what—"

Looking up at me through her fingers, she sucks in a breath. "You know full well what a manipulative cunt he can be."

"What did he do?" Fury starts to seep its way through my body. The vibes I'm getting from her aren't good, and I know that whatever happened is going to make me even more glad the fucker's dead.

"Let's just say he used my weakness at the time against me."

A low growl rumbles up my throat as I stand with my hands on the desk. My fingers grip onto the edge, turning my knuckles white as I try to keep my head together. Just the thought of him manipulating someone else I care about makes me want to do some damage. I pin her with a look that has her sitting up straight in the chair. Tears fill her eyes, but I can tell she's fighting to keep them from falling. Her bottom lip trembles as she continues twisting her hands together.

"I...I can't, Ben."

The sound of the office buzzer rings out as we stare at each other. My imagination is running wild right now. There's not a lot I wouldn't say Nick was capable of. I need her to tell me exactly what it is so I can stop thinking the worst.

"What did he do?" She flinches at my cold tone, and I regret it instantly. I don't want my anger at him to push her away, but I can't help it.

"I...I slept with him."

"You what?" I roar.

"I didn't have a choice." Her voice is quiet and weak. There's so much more to this than she's letting on. Walking around the desk, I pull her from the chair and wrap my arms around her trembling body.

"It's okay," I say softly when she fights to get away. She must realise she's got no chance of overpowering me, because she soon gives up and relaxes into me for a few seconds.

It's only the click of the door opening that has us breaking apart.

"He's just in here," Betty says, gesturing someone inside.

CHAPTER NINE

MY BROWS DRAW together as I briefly wonder who'd be looking for me, but I soon get my answer when four people I was not expecting appear from behind Betty.

"Holy shit."

The realisation that my worlds are about to collide renders me speechless as I stare at my two best friends and their girls.

"Surprise." Liv comes over to give me a quick hug. "You must be Lauren." She says, pushing me aside when she spots Erica hiding behind me. "It's so good to finally meet you."

"Oh, what? No...no. I'm Erica."

Turning, I can't help but laugh at the look of disgust on Erica's face at the thought of her being

Lauren. "No need to look so horrified. You know you'd love it." I give her a wink and she makes a show of pretending to throw up.

"There's not enough money in the world for me to go there, *mate*."

Dec and Liam stifle a laugh while Liv looks between the two of us. "I think we're going to get on," she says to Erica.

I'm reminded of the similarities between the two women. Both have been my saviours at different points in my life. I'll never be able to repay them for the support they've given me.

"What the hell are you guys doing here?" I eventually manage to ask, once my shock has worn off.

"Liv thought you might need a night out."

"You came all this way for a night out?"

"Yeah, well...we might miss you," Liam says, looking a little awkward.

"It's not same without you crashing around the house. You sounded like you needed some fun on the phone the other day, so I've organised a surprise."

Raising an eyebrow, I wait for Liv to elaborate, but she makes a show of zipping her lips shut. "All I can say is that tomorrow night you're going to love us more than you already do. The only thing we need from you is the name of a club for after."

"No strip club, please."

Both Dec and Liam's eyes widen, reminding me that the guy they've known for the last six years isn't the one standing in front of them. "Shut up, you fucking love it, BJ."

"BJ?" Erica pipes up with a smirk playing at her lips.

Falling down onto the chair behind me, I realise for the first time just how different my two lives are. Bringing them together is going to be weird as fuck.

Dec and Liam's eyes burn into my skin. I can practically feel them trying to work all of this out while the soft whisper of plotting female voices at the other side of the room floats around.

"So, this is the family business then?" Dec asks, looking around the office. "It looks pretty flash for a builder's office."

"That's because it's not just any builder's office." I give them both a brief run-down of what we do...or at least what we did before I disappeared.

"Have you guys got somewhere to stay or..." I trail off. The thought of taking them home and immersing them in my life here makes me feel more on edge than I've experienced in a long time. I try not to think about why that might be, but I know all too well that I'm worried what they'll think about meeting the 'real' me. The act I've put on around them became second nature. I hate that I've lied to them about my past and where I came from, but it felt right at the time.

"No, we thought we'd sort something once we were here."

"Do you…uh…if you want, I'm sure Mum wouldn't mind…uh…"

"We'd love to meet your mum, Ben," Nicole says softly. "Then we can always find a hotel later, right?" She looks to the others, who all nod, and I breathe a sigh of relief.

"I'll meet you out the front," I say, as everyone files out of the office.

"Are you okay?" I bend down slightly so I can look into Erica's downcast eyes.

"I'm a fighter, Ben. I've had no choice."

"That doesn't make any of this okay." Seeing tears starting to swim in her eyes again, I pull her against my chest and squeeze tight. Probably a little too tightly I realise when she starts to complain.

"Go and spend some time with your friends."

"Come with us?"

"No. I've got loads to do here. Someone needs to

keep this place from going under." Guilt hits me that it's been left to Erica to take the lead. "No, don't look at me like that. I didn't say it to make you feel bad. You go and do your thing. Me and the business will be here when you're ready." I'm hesitant, but she soon starts attempting to push me towards the door. "We've all got a lot of work on our hands, but we've got a little time. Go."

"Okay, but we'll be talking, Erica. Soon." She tries to cover her fear, but I can see it in her eyes. "Everything will be okay." With a small smile, I leave her in the doorway of the office. I'm not sure either of us believe the words that just came from my mouth.

After joining the others outside, we head for home. Liv insists on coming with me while Dec follows behind on the short drive to the house where I grew up.

I know she's only concerned, but when Liv starts asking about Lauren, I keep my answers as short as possible. She sees through it though.

"What are you hiding?"

Glancing over, I find her staring at me, trying to figure me out. Feeling uncomfortable, I shift in my seat and try to change the subject.

"Dec and Nic were able to get away from the shack then?"

"Stop it. Stop trying to distract me. I just want to help, and I can't do that if you won't talk to me."

I bite my tongue and refrain from telling her that I managed just fine before she turned up and insisted on trying to find out more about me.

"I slept with her. Happy now?"

Liv gasps. "But you said she had a—"

"I know. Trust me, I know. But it...it just happened."

"I told you she didn't hate you," she says with a laugh, trying to lighten the mood.

"No, I'm pretty sure she does. I'm also pretty sure she regrets every second with me last night." I let out a long sigh as I recall her words this morning.

Liv places her hand on my shoulder and squeezes gently. "Everything will be okay."

"How can you be so positive all the time?"

"I just have a feeling. Fucking hell, is this where you live?" Her tone suddenly changes as I pull up to the gates in front of the house I used to call home and they open slowly. "You're rich?"

"I'm not, no. My mum is though, I guess. The only money I have is that arsehole's dirty money."

A shiver runs down my spine as I'm reminded of some of the things Erica said to me earlier. The reality is that Mum might not have anything. My stomach twists and I feel sick at the thought of him leaving her and Lauren with nothing. After all the bullshit he pulled, that would just be the tip of the iceberg. I always suspected that he only married Mum to get his hands on the business and the money that came with it. Him leaving it on the edge of bankruptcy is only more evidence that I was right all along.

Mum's car is sitting in the drive as I expected, but I suck in a breath when I see another next to it.

"Shit."

"What's wrong?"

"Lauren's here. I thought she'd gone back home."

"We can go somewhere else. Find a hotel and meet later..."

She trails off and I look over at her. She's been nothing but incredible since we met. I'll feel even more of an arsehole than I usually do if I turn them all away now. They've come here because they want to help. It's time I stopped running and embraced the real me.

"No, it's fine. Come on."

I jump out of the car as Dec brings his van to a stop behind me. Liam nods and I give him a weak smile.

"What are you so worried about? The guys will

love you whether you're surfing in Devon or running an empire in London. Just chill, yeah?"

"Well, this wasn't quite what I was expecting. It's practically a fucking mansion," Dec says, helping Nicole from the van.

"I guess," I mutter. I always knew we were well off; but having gone to private school with even more privileged and wealthy kids, my house never seemed all that impressive.

They all follow me in, stopping to take their shoes off, unlike me who just traipses through towards the kitchen.

"Are you sure that's the best way to go about it?" I hear Mum ask as I get to the doorway.

Lauren's mouth opens to respond, but before she gets a chance, she must sense my presence. Her eyes find mine and anger twists her features. "I need to leave."

"Lauren, this is your home."

"No, Jenny. It's your home." She flicks another look my way. "And his. It's best I get out of your way."

"Thank you, Lauren. For everything. I know your dad's no longer..." she trails off, sadness clouding her features. "Just...don't be a stranger."

I watch as they embrace while the others come to

a stop behind me.

When Lauren turns, it's with tears filling her eyes. She keeps her head down as she walks my way, but at the very last minute, she looks up.

There are so many things I need to say to her, mostly apologies, but all the words stay on the end of my tongue as our eyes hold. She looks tired. Exhausted. I know it's not all my fault, but I feel the weight of it pressing down on my chest nonetheless.

The atmosphere is heavy around us as we stare at each other. Reaching my hand forward, I brush my fingers against hers gently. Her eyelids flicker as our connection hits her, but she rights herself all too quickly and pulls her hand away.

Someone behind me clears their throat, and I'm reminded that they're there.

"Shit. Mum, Lauren, these are my friends." Turning, I introduce each of them. It's not escaped me that I'm yet to fully explain to either Mum or Lauren where I've been and what I've been doing over the past few years.

"N-nice to meet you. I'm sorry, but I need to..." Lauren's voice cracks and she all but runs towards the front door.

"Lauren...wait," Liv calls, shocking the fuck out

of me—and Lauren, too, if the look on her face when she turns is anything to go by.

Liv races over and leans in to have a private conversation with a woman she's never met before as if they're best friends.

Narrowing my eyes, I watch them for a few seconds before Mum welcomes everyone in and offers them drinks. Dec, Liam and Nicole just about manage to squeeze past me and into the room as I stand stock still, trying to figure out what Liv's saying.

I'm still staring when she gives Lauren a quick hug and watches her leave the house. She then turns to me and smiles like she was expecting me to be watching, but comes walking over as if nothing weird just happened.

Reaching out, I grab her forearm as she tries to walk past me.

"What the hell was that?"

"It was nothing for you to worry about." She gives me a wink before walking farther into the room and introducing herself to my mum.

I watch from the corner of the room as my friends and Mum sit around the table talking as if they've known each other for years.

I was a little worried what state we might find

Mum in when we got here, but she looks good. Better than I've seen since I came home. She's abandoned her glass of wine in favour of coffee with everyone else, and her smile is wide and genuine as she listens to Dec talk about Devon and what I've been doing.

"Yeah, he's an incredible surfer."

"Is that right, Ben?" Her question drags me from my own head, and I walk over and pull a chair out.

"I'm okay. Dec and Liam are way better than me. I'm not really built for a board."

"Yeah, you have grown a little," Mum says with a laugh. "He's been back days and I know nothing. Tell me everything my baby's been up to."

"Everything?" Dec asks, looking over at me with an evil smile playing at his lips.

"No, she doesn't need to know everything."

I've no idea why I was so nervous about this. I might have thought I was putting on an act in Devon, but I think maybe my friends have always seen through it.

For the first time in a very, very long time, I actually enjoy spending a night in this house. It's filled with warmth and laughter. It's something I'm sure hasn't really happened since my dad died, but suddenly it's a home again. It's just a shame one person is missing. The seat next to me at the table is empty, and so is a huge part of me, despite being surrounded by these incredible people.

"Have you already got accommodation sorted for the night?" Mum asks.

"No. It was all a little last minute. We—"

"Stay here," Mum says quickly, cutting Liv off.

"Oh no. We don't want to impose. We know you've got a lot going on right now."

"Don't be silly. I won't take no for an answer. It's been so wonderful having Ben's friends here and hearing about my boy. I couldn't possibly allow you to leave. Let me go and make sure the guest rooms are ready for visitors." Mum gets up and quickly leaves the room. I can't help but think her having people to look after is going to help pull her from the dark hole she was falling into.

"Your mum's lovely, B...Ben." Dec's lips twist weirdly as he tries to wrap them around my real name. "BJ was never your nickname was it?"

"No. Until you, I was always Ben."

"You should have said something."

"Honestly, I needed the separation from here." Guilt hits me again at hiding so much of myself from my best friends.

"Yeah, I think I'm starting to understand that. Why did you never tell us any of this?"

"I didn't leave under good circumstances. The less I had to think about it, the better."

"Why did you leave?"

I smile at Liv, who's kept my secret even without me being there. "My stepdad made me."

"Made you?" Nicole asks with her brows drawn together. "Why?"

"I fell in love with his daughter and he found out. He paid me to—"

"He what?" comes from behind us. Turning, I find Mum clinging onto the doorframe for support, her eyes wide as she stares at me, willing me to tell her that I'm lying. "Ben? Is that true?"

Letting out a breath, I look over at my mum's distressed face. "Of course it's true. Did you really think I'd leave you both willingly?"

She sags against the wall, and both Liam and I are up and off our chairs to catch her.

"He paid you?" she whispers, looking up at me with sad eyes once we've got her settled on a chair.

"He did. But it wasn't the money that forced me to go."

"W-what was it?"

Looking up to the ceiling, I battle with how much I want to tell her. I know she deserves the truth, but the last thing I want to do is hurt her. She's already suffered enough pain. I look around at all the sets of eyes staring at me, and I feel awful for her finding out this way. We should have had this conversation in private, not in front of people she hardly knows. But I can't help feel that it's better to get it all out in the open.

Looking away from her, I swallow and consider my words. "He threatened you and Lauren. He said he had enough evidence that you…hadn't been faithful. That he could take everything." Mum's face pales and she swallows nervously; it's all I need to know it's true. "If I didn't walk away, he was going to take the business, the house, everything, and leave you with nothing. Both of you. I couldn't risk it. After Dad, I just couldn't—"

"You really loved her, didn't you?" she manages to croak out, taking the focus away from her.

Feeling everyone's eyes turn on me, I swallow down the lump that's growing in my throat. "I still do."

"You need to fight for her, Ben."

Not able to look into Mum's heartbroken eyes any longer, I push the chair out behind me, swipe a beer from the fridge, and head out to the garden. Watching her reaction to the truth about her husband on top of Erica's confession this afternoon is just getting a bit much.

Knocking the cap off on the edge of the table, I fall back onto one of the chairs and tip the bottle to my lips. The cool liquid goes down too easily, making old habits to drown everything out so bloody tempting.

I've no idea how much time passes before the sound of the doors opening pulls me from my own head. When I look up, Dec and Liam are heading my way with more beer.

They both drop down beside me and pass me a new bottle. Nothing's said as we all open them and take a swig.

"The girls are with your mum," Liam says, and my stomach twists.

"Fuck. I should go—" I go to stand but a hand on my shoulder stops me.

"They've got it covered. Stop worrying about everyone else for a few minutes and just take a breath."

I do as he suggests and drag in a few good lungfuls of air. "The business is going under. This place could end up repossessed and—"

"And we're going to sort it. You won't lose any of this."

"No, no, you don't—"

"Enough," Dec snaps. "All you've done since the day we met is help me. You practically rebuilt my house from the ground up. You supported me starting the business. You were there for me with everything with Nicole. We will not allow you to do this alone, Ben."

The determination on their faces chokes me up. Fear that the tears stinging my eyes might just escape if I acknowledge their support means I tip my bottle to my lips instead.

"Thank you," I say eventually.

"Whatever you need," Liam agrees before silence surrounds us once again. We're guys, we don't really talk about feelings and shit, but I don't need it. They're here; that's all I need to know that they mean everything Dec just said.

We've almost drunk our way through the bottles the guys brought out when the sound of the doors opening floats around us. Nic and Liv step out and walk over to join us.

"Is she okay?"

"She's gone to bed. She's exhausted."

They both give me sad smiles—it's their way of saying that she's not okay. I really wish that conversation about Nick could have happened in private, but I guess it's too late now.

We stay out on the decking, drinking and chatting long into the night. Once we decide to hit the sack, I follow both the couples up the stairs and watch as they go into their rooms for the night.

There's a stabbing pain in my heart as I head towards my own room alone. Forgoing my bedroom door, I push down the handle on the one opposite. Nothing in this room is like I remember, but just knowing it's where she used to be brings me some kind of comfort. Sitting myself down on the edge of the bed, I think about how I could have handled all of this differently. I thought not telling Lauren about her dad the second I got here was for the best. Allow her to mourn the man she thought he was, to say goodbye to the father she believed she had, before I hit her with the truth. But after the way Mum found out tonight, I'm starting to question that decision.

Knowing that sitting here wallowing isn't helping anyone, I get up to leave, but the sound of giggling coming from one of the guest rooms stops me. Will any of this get any easier?

Knocking softly on Mum's door, I push it open and poke my head inside.

"It's okay, I'm awake," she says quietly.

Walking in, I make my way over to the bed and sit myself beside her.

"I'm so sorry, Mum. My intention wasn't to hurt anyone in all of this. I was trying to do what I thought was best for you."

"Shush, now," she soothes, placing her tiny hand on my forearm. "You should have stood up for yourself and what you wanted."

"I couldn't do that to you. The business and this house are the only bits of Dad you had left. I just—"

"They're just things, Ben. No matter where I live, or where I work, your dad will always be with me." Tears sting my eyes and she brings her hand to her chest. "Your dad was the love of my life. Even to this day he holds my heart in his hands. I don't need to be in this house to remember him. You should have fought. If I'd have known, I'd have told you the same thing back then. Nick was ruthless. Everyone seems to think I wasn't aware of the kind of man he was, but I experienced it better than anyone."

My fists clench as I vividly remember some of their more heated arguments. I used to hide just out of sight waiting for the hand he raised to come down on her. I never witnessed it, but I'd put money on the fact some of Mum's *illnesses* were due to his fists.

"I really fucking hate him. He took everything

from me. I wasn't going to allow him to do that to both of you, too."

"Oh, baby." Mum tries to wrap her arms around my shoulders, but I'm not the baby she remembers, and her arms nowhere near meet. She ends up with her head resting on my chest as I hold her to me. "We did lose everything. We lost you."

Thank fuck she's looking down; it means she misses the fight I lose with my tears as she sobs her own.

I angrily wipe at my eyes, frustrated with myself that I've allowed him to break me.

When Mum does pull her head up and look at me, she doesn't miss the emotion written all over my face. She places her hand softly on my cheek and stares into my eyes. I suddenly feel like a little boy again.

"You and Lauren were made for each other. I knew that the first time I caught you together. There was something about the two of you when you were close, an unbreakable connection. It was just like your dad and I had. You've no idea how I feel, knowing I played a part in ruining that. I knew about the two of you, but I didn't do anything to help. There are so many things I could have done. I—"

"Don't, Mum. It's too late now. What's done is

done. She has every right not to want anything to do with me after what I did."

"That's just it though, Ben. She's still angry. That's a good thing."

"How?"

"It means she still cares. It means it's not over, no matter what she might try to tell you." My heart starts to race as her words settle in. "Don't give up." Reaching up, she places a kiss to my cheek before settling herself back into bed. "*Never* give up, Ben."

I leave soon after, but Mum's words stay with me as I lie in my own bed, staring at the ceiling, waiting for sleep to claim me. I wonder if what she said is true. Would things have been different if she'd have said something? Somehow, I really doubt it. Nick still would have found a way to get what he wanted. He might have just gone about it differently.

CHAPTER TEN

"MORNING," I grunt, walking into the kitchen to find both Nic and Liv cooking up something that smells fantastic.

"I hope you don't mind. We raided the cupboards."

"Knock yourselves out."

I get myself a coffee before refilling Dec and Liam's, who are sitting at the table watching their girls. Both of them have freshly fucked smug smiles on their faces.

"Which one of your headboards was banging all night?"

"Ours," Dec and Liam say in unison as the girls deny everything while turning a nice shade of pink.

"Mum said you can stay, not that you could turn

the place into a knocking shop," I say with a laugh, falling down onto a chair with the guys.

"Oh please, like you didn't get up to all sorts here when you were a teenager." Everyone falls silent and realisation dawns on Nicole as to what she just said. "Oh shit, I'm sorry. I didn't think."

"It's fine. You're right, though. I've done my fair share of sneaking around in this place."

"Is that right?" Mum asks with a wink as she joins us.

"It's probably best we change the conversation." Mum laughs, and it's the first time since I've been back that I've seen her smile meet her eyes.

She walks over and gives me a hug. "Everything's going to be okay. You'll see." I nod at her because I don't want to ruin her good mood, but right now I'm getting fed up of everyone telling me that.

We've just finished eating when my phone vibrates in my pocket. Pulling it out, my brows pull together at seeing Liv's name on the screen.

"What the hell is this?"

"It's your surprise."

"You got Rita fucking Ora tickets for tonight?"

"I did."

"How? It sold out months ago?" I ask, totally

forgetting any attempt to cover up my slight addiction to the singer.

"It doesn't matter. All that matters is that I got them."

"You're a fucking legend." I jump from the chair and have her in my arms in seconds. I spin her around as she squeals and the others all laugh.

"So you want to go then?" she asks as she tries to stand steady once I've lowered her to her feet.

"Fucking right I do. I seriously can't fucking believe this." The smile splitting my face hurts as I stare down my phone once again. I'm going to the fucking O2 tonight to see Rita fucking Ora. What did I do to deserve friends like these?

"This is so fucking awesome."

"It's good to see you smile again, dude," Liam says, clapping me on the back.

I guess that's why the muscles in my face are aching so much; they haven't really been used a lot lately.

"So what's the plan, then? We've got hours until the concert. There's no way I can sit around here waiting."

The girls announce that they'd like to go shopping, so we end up spending the afternoon walking up and down Oxford Street while Dec and Liam carry their bags.

We have a great afternoon, but seeing the four of them together is only a massive reminder of what I don't have. I'd give just about anything to follow Lauren around each and every shop, holding her bags and giving her my advice, which of course would be that she always looked incredible.

I tried phoning Erica before we left the house this morning, but all my calls went straight to voicemail. I may be bouncing about what tonight is going to hold, but everything she told me yesterday isn't far from my mind. I intend on making the most of having my friends here, but I need to find out just how bad a shape the business is in, and even more, I need to find out what exactly Nick did to Erica.

Before I know it, Dec, Liam and I are all sitting in Mum's living room, waiting for the girls to appear.

"Seriously, how did Liv get those tickets?" I ask Liam.

"I think someone was selling them on or something. Cost us all a damn fortune."

Guilt twists my stomach that they're all out of pocket trying to cheer me up. "I can pay for them all."

"Don't be stupid. This is on us," Dec argues as we hear footsteps and giggling descending the stairs.

"I think I've changed my mind about going out," Liam announces the second Liv walks into the room wearing a little black dress.

He immediately sweeps her into his arms, followed by Dec who does the same to Nic. I once again feel like the gooseberry of the group. Awkwardly, I manage to squeeze past them and walk out to the driveway with my head down.

Mum's words from yesterday ring in my ears. Is it too late? Is what she said true? Are we over? Has she really moved on?

Once they've finished manhandling each other, they join me and we head towards the tube station to take us into the city centre. Liam and Dec are oblivious, but I get sympathetic smiles from the girls. They seem to have a better understanding of how painful it is seeing them all loved up and happy.

Nicole and Liv choose a popular gastro pub for dinner before heading towards the O2.

As we stand outside waiting in line, I'm more grateful than I think I've ever been for a distraction. The prospect of spending an hour or two watching Rita up on stage is enough for me to push everything with Mum, Lauren, Erica, and the business to the back of my mind. I know as soon as tonight's over that I'll have to deal with them all once again, but for now, I'm just going to enjoy myself.

The seats are fucking incredible for last minute, second-hand tickets.

"You're something else, you know that?" I shout to Liv as the support act takes to the stage. "You've no idea how badly I need this."

"I think I do." She winks at me, and I'm reminded of everything she went through recently and how she knows better than anyone what a good distraction from reality can do.

Wrapping my arm around her shoulder, I kiss the top of her head. Liam smiles at me from next to her and I nod back. These guys have been my family for the past six years, and they mean more to me than I think they'll ever understand. They were exactly what I needed in those first few months after leaving London, and the fact that they're here now when I need them is everything to me.

Feeling a little choked up, I'm glad when the band leave the stage and the crowd erupts in excitement for the lady of the night.

Butterflies explode in my stomach as the anticipation builds. The only thing that would make tonight better would be if Lauren were here to experience it with me. I look to my left, at the random lady patiently staring at the stage, and my excitement wanes.

I missed her so fucking much when I was in Devon, but being here, with her practically in touching distance, is even worse.

The concert is more than I ever thought it might be. I've wanted to see her live ever since I first heard her voice on the radio a few years ago. My desire only got worse when I Googled her and discovered she looked as good as she sounded. I've taken plenty of stick over the years about my obsession, but I couldn't give a fuck. She's hot and her music is sweet, so what's not to love?

The whole time she's singing, I completely forget about all the bullshit surrounding me, all the unknowns about my life. I embrace every second of the freedom she provides me with. I breathe that little bit easier with her voice filling my ears.

"So?" Liv asks as we walk from the arena once the show is over. "Was it everything you always dreamed of?" I don't miss the little smirk on her lips.

"It was incredible. Thank you so much."

"You're welcome."

"Please tell me we're not heading home yet." I'm

buzzing after that and really not ready to deal with reality.

"No, we're heading to a club."

Liv takes the lead and we follow her down to the tube station and further into the city.

The second we emerge from the underground, I know exactly where we're going. I remember the little chat she had with Erica yesterday, and I realise they were planning this night. Erica never wanted to go anywhere but Fire back in the day.

As we approach the club I used to know so well, I notice some obvious changes. The orange Fire signage is long gone, replaced with a more upmarket look. It's now called The Avenue, and everything's black and chrome. From the few people outside, it no longer looks to be filled with drunk students and has a slightly higher quality clientele, something I'm relieved about.

"This place looks nice," Nicole says from behind me as we queue up to get in.

They chat away, but I don't hear most of it. The anticipation that's running through me is the only thing I can focus on. If Erica had something to do with these plans, then there's a very good chance she's here...and Lauren could be too.

My heart thunders in my chest as the bouncer

gestures for us to enter. I immediately take the stairs up to the second floor. I've no idea if it would still be Erica's choice, but it's the only thing I have to go on if we're going to find her.

Dec orders us all shots of whiskey and I quickly down mine, not wanting to take my eyes off my surroundings for a second.

Tingles run up and down my spine. I know she's here somewhere. I just need to find her. My mouth waters as my imagination runs wild. I vividly remember us dancing here, the way her body felt against mine. How badly I needed her that night.

It's only a few seconds before the sea of people in front of me parts just right and my eyes land on her. She's wearing a deep red dress that's wrapped around her perfect curves. My fingers twitch to feel them once again as my eyes run down her long, exposed legs to her black high heels.

Fuck me.

Making my way back up over every delicious curve that's moving in time with the music, I eventually get to her blonde hair that's pulled away from her slim neck and piled on top of her head.

I'm getting closer before my brain's even registered that my legs are moving. I'm only a few feet away when someone steps out from the crowd, places their hands on her hips, and pulls her backwards.

My fists clench as my temperature soars. I stare at where he's touching her and fight my need to rip his hands away.

Raising my eyes, I take in his perfectly pressed white shirt, braces, and then his overly gelled hair. If I didn't hate him when I saw him touching Lauren at the funeral, then I do now.

Every muscle in my body tenses as I watch their hips grind together.

"Whoa, dude, what's...oh!" Dec stands beside me, watching the same car crash that I am.

"I need more fucking whiskey for this." Turning, I walk back up to the bar and order another round of drinks.

"Hey, we didn't think you were coming," I hear a familiar voice say behind me.

Spinning around, I find a very happy Erica smiling at me, but when I lift my eyes over her shoulder, I find the same anger on Lauren's face that I'm sure was on mine not so long ago.

"I think I should leave."

"Don't you fucking dare," Erica warns. The vicious look in her eyes has me rooted to the spot. "Ben, you remember Danni, right?" she says when

Lauren's friend comes to a stop beside her. A similar hatred fills her eyes as she looks me up and down.

"Danni," I say with a nod.

"Hmm, look what the cat dragged in," she slurs, curling her lip up in disgust. "You've got some nerve showing your face here, you know that?"

"Danni, stop, please," Lauren begs, coming to stand beside her best friend.

"And this is Joe," Erica interrupts.

I hold her stare for a few seconds, so she knows just how unhappy I am about this before I look up.

I find him staring down at me with pure hatred pouring from his eyes. I take a step forward, ready to do whatever it takes to show this douchebag that he has something that belongs to me.

"Don't even think about it," Lauren seethes, jumping between us.

I stop millimetres from her body. Her heat seeps into me. It's almost enough to make me forget about the man who thinks she's his. Mum was right last night. Lauren still cares, so everything is still to play for.

It's not until her hands land on my chest that I pull my eyes from her *boyfriend*. My lip curls at just the thought alone.

"Step away, Ben," she warns. With her shoes on,

she's much taller than usual. It wouldn't take much for me to lean down and take her lips right now. The idea has my mouth watering for another taste of her.

Narrowing my eyes, I can't stop the words falling from my lips. "You know you want me to fight for you. I can sense it." Lowering my head to her ear, I whisper, "I can smell it. He doesn't make you scream like I do, and you fucking know it."

Her hand connects with my cheek, and it stings like a motherfucker. Pressing my palm to my burning skin, I look down at her. Her eyes are alight with anger and her chests heaves as she stares back at me.

"I fucking hate you," she spits.

"No, baby. You just hate that I'm not fucking you."

"That's enough, Ben," Erica shouts, grabbing my arm and trying to turn me away to stop me saying anything else.

"It's nowhere fucking near enough. He needs to realise she's mine before I make him regret ever touching her."

"Whoa, calm down, caveman. I know I told you to fight for her, but that wasn't quite what I meant."

I'm ushered over towards the bar and a glass of whiskey appears in front of me.

When I look up, I'm met by the concerned looks

of my best friends. I don't need to meet their eyes to know I just fucked up.

"Are you going to play nice, or do I have to send you home?" Erica asks with a hard stare and her hands on her hips.

"I'm fine. I'm fine."

I can tell none of them believe me. Hell, I'm not sure I believe me, but I'm not walking out of here and leaving them to grind it up on the dance floor without a care in the world.

Downing my drink, I grab Erica's hand and pull her into the crowd. Lauren and that prick aren't the only ones who've got moves.

I know everyone's watching as I twist Erica around in front of me, but there's only one set of eyes that are burning hatred into me.

Erica's body is stiff when I force her against my chest and start dancing. "What the hell are you doing? If you want to make her jealous, using me probably isn't the best idea."

"You're right." Pushing her away, I glance around. It doesn't take long before I find a woman watching me. She's not my type in any way, but right now, that's the last thing that matters. I pull her stick thin body against mine and together we move in time with the music.

She's clearly drunk and more than willing. Guilt starts to eat at me that I'm taking advantage of her, but I tell myself that I have no intention of doing anything more than dance.

I pin her hips against mine and she moves easily with me. The others join me and lose themselves with their other halves. Joe pulls Lauren to the edge of our group and my teeth grind as I watch his hands run down her back until they land on her arse.

My fingers squeeze the woman pressed up against me and it gives her the wrong idea. Her hand slides up my chest and wraps around the back of my neck.

My eyes stay on Lauren as the woman presses her lips to mine. It takes a second or two, but the moment she notices, she stops moving. Joe stares down at her before following her eye line and also finding me.

He turns back to her, and I do the same, but it's too late. She's already gone.

Forcing the woman pressed against me away, I rush in the direction where Lauren disappeared.

"I don't think so." I'm toe-to-toe with Joe. We're a similar height and build, but I'm confident I could take him if need be. He looks like a fucking IT geek with his black-rimmed glasses and slicked back hair after all.

"What the fuck do you know about anything?"

"More than you fucking know. You've already caused her enough pain, don't you think?" he asks, but I've already pushed him away in my need to get to her. "Let her go, Ben. It's too late."

I hear other calls from behind me, but I pay them no attention.

Racing down the stairs, I search for her, but there's no sign of her blonde hair or red dress.

"Go in the toilets and find her," I demand when Erica follows me.

"She's gone, Ben. Come back and get a drink?" Hope fills her eyes that tonight might not be a total bust, but it's too late. The damage has already been done.

"I'm going home. Give this to the others for a taxi later."

She shoves the handful of cash back at me and turns away without saying anything. *Great, I've pissed someone else off.*

I don't manage to get a taxi before the others come rushing from the club.

"What the fuck are you doing?" Liam shouts as he walks over. He doesn't stop until he's right in my face. "You want to fight? You want to hit someone? Come on, then. Take what you need."

"I'm not going to fucking hit you."

"Why not?"

"You haven't done anything to deserve it."

"And *he* has?"

He stumbles back when I push his shoulders, but Dec manages to catch him before he hits the pavement.

"Fuck you. FUCK YOU!" I bellow at no one in particular. Running my hands over my face, I rest them on my head and look up to the dark, cloud filled sky. It's angry, like there could be a storm any moment.

I suck in a few breaths in the hope of calming my racing heart and raging temper.

When I finally get a hold of myself and turn to the others, they're standing on the pavement, looking totally lost. Guilt engulfs me. They came here to try to cheer me up, and this is what I subject them to.

I'm a joke.

My life is a fucking joke.

"Come on. Let's get you home," Liv says softly, lacing her fingers with mine and pulling me towards a taxi idling at the curb.

CHAPTER ELEVEN

"HOW ARE YOU FEELING? Your friends said you had a bit of an eventful night," Mum says when I eventually drag my hungover arse into the kitchen sometime after lunch the next day.

"Like shit."

"Sit down, I'll get you a coffee. The others have gone into the city for the day. They didn't want to disturb you."

I watch as Mum faffs about. She looks better again today. I'm hoping that finding out the truth, although painful, has done her some good.

"Here. Chris is coming around in a little bit with Nick's will. Lauren's coming too." Dread sits heavily in my stomach. I was such a dick to her in the club. Mum must be able to read my thoughts, because after regarding me for a few seconds, she asks, "What did you do?"

"I wasn't very nice to her last night. She was at the club with Joe and—"

"Oh. I think you and Joe would get on, you know. You're really quite similar."

"Yeah, it seems we have similar tastes," I mutter.

Mum bites down on her bottom lip and considers her next words carefully. "Not all that similar," she says eventually. I don't get a chance to question what she means, because the doorbell rings.

Mum gets up, stops at the mirror in the hallway to smooth down her hair, and answers the door.

Chris' deep voice filters down to me along with Mum's laughter. The sound warms my heart.

"Afternoon, Ben," Chris calls as he enters the room, and I wince. "Good night?"

"Something like that," I mutter, regretting the amount of whiskey I consumed before finally crashing out.

"We're just waiting for Lauren and then we can get to it. What's that look for?" Mum asks Chris when concern washes over his face.

"It's just...not what I was expecting."

Mum swallows before turning to make Chris a coffee. "Whatever it is, we can deal with it, Chris. He didn't break us when he was alive, and he sure won't do it when he's dead."

It's the first time I've ever heard Mum say anything less than positive about her late husband. Maybe she was right with what she said the other day, and she was more aware of his ways than she let on.

Mum's just put Chris' coffee down when the sound of the front door slamming echoes through the house.

I hold my breath as her footsteps echo down the hallway. It all comes out in a rush when she finally appears in the doorway. She's wearing a pair of skinny jeans and an oversized hoodie, her hair's pulled back from her make-up free, tired face, but it's her eyes that make my body ache to get up. Her usual light-blue is dark and rimmed with redness that only comes from hours of crying.

My fingers grip the bottom of the chair to keep me in place. She's staring daggers at me. Getting up and giving her a hug is the last thing she wants right now.

"Good afternoon, sweetheart. Would you like tea?"

"Please."

"Take a seat. I'll be right with you all."

Lauren takes the farthest seat away from me and I almost laugh. If she thinks that's going to keep me away, she's got another think coming.

The wood of my chair legs screeches against the tiled floor. Her eyes fly up to me and hold a warning—one I'm about to ignore.

She tenses as I pull a chair out next to her and drop down. Resting my arm over her backrest, she sits bolt upright so we don't touch.

Leaning forward so Mum and Chris can't eavesdrop, I whisper in her ear, "I'm sorry about last night. It was uncalled for. It taught me something though." Turning to me, she narrows her eyes in question. "You still want me."

Standing, she goes to leave, but I'm faster. Wrapping my hand around her forearm, I hold her in place.

"Ben? Lauren? Is everything okay?"

"Please can we just get this over with?"

"Sure. Chris, are you ready?"

"Yes," he says hesitantly.

After ripping her arm from my grasp, Lauren sits back down beside me, folds her arms over her chest and waits for what Chris has to say.

He talks through all the waffle and formalities. He seems to really drag out the inevitable, that Mum will get everything. I assume he's left something for Lauren, but why Chris can't just come out and say it is beyond me.

"So, Nick has requested that in the case of his passing, this house and the business are left to...Ben."

"What?" both Lauren and I say at the same time.

"He's left everything to the man who walked away when things got too hard? What the fuck?" Anger vibrates from her as she stands. "What about Jenny and me?"

"I'm sorry, sweetheart. Ben is the only person named."

"This is bullshit." We all stare at her as she turns on her heel and storms from the room, and soon after, the house.

"Well, that went well," Chris mutters sadly.

"He really left everything to Ben?" Mum asks, her face twisted in confusion. It's in that moment that realisation hits.

"Well, he wouldn't leave that kind of disaster to someone he actually likes, would he?"

"What do you mean?"

"The business is about to go under, and this place has been re-mortgaged to the hilt. It's clearly his idea of a sick joke. He's left all his debt and dirty dealings for me to attempt to sort out."

"What are you talking about? The business is doing fine. Lauren does the accounts; she would have said if something was wrong."

"I don't think it's that simple, Mum. He's been cooking the books along with fuck knows what else."

"How do you know this?"

"I don't know the details, but he's been using Erica to hide what he's been up to."

"Motherfucker," Chris grunts.

Mum just sits there in total shock. "Am I going to lose the house?" she asks eventually. I expect her to break down, but there's no emotion.

"Not if I have anything to do with it. Is that it, Chris?"

"For now, yes. We'll need to sort out paperwork soon though."

"Okay, well, you've got my number." Draining my coffee, I stand from the table and head in the direction Lauren went not so long ago. My hangover is suddenly forgotten. I've got more important things to worry about, like keeping a roof over Mum's head.

The anger that had erupted within me at learning what that motherfucker had left me is raging by the time I pull up outside Johnson & Son's office.

My granddad started the business from his spare bedroom. It was my dad who moved everything here.

He started with just a small corner of the floor, but as the business grew, so did the office space. We now take up the entire second floor of the building—although, I doubt that's going to continue, depending on what I find when I start digging into my inheritance.

The crisp early autumn air chills my skin as I walk the short distance from where I manage to find a parking space to the office building.

I'm expecting it to be empty seeing as it's a Sunday, so I'm surprised when I push the door open and find the lights on.

"I just don't get it. Dad hated Ben—why would he leave it all to him?" The sound of her soft, emotional voice has goosebumps erupting across my skin. There's so much she doesn't know. So much that prick hid from her.

Pushing the door open wider, I walk towards them, ready to get everything out in the open.

I'm not surprised to see it's Erica she's talking to. Lauren's leaning back against her desk, totally oblivious that they have company. Erica, on the other hand, spots me immediately over Lauren's shoulder. Her eyes widen in surprise.

"I just don't understand why he'd do this to Jenny."

"Lauren...I..." Erica stutters, her eyes still on me.

"We need to explain a few things to you." Lauren's body visibly tenses as my voice fills the space around us.

"We?" Erica asks, fear draining the colour from her face.

"Yes, Erica. It's time."

"I don't want to listen to anything you have to say," she spits.

"Tough. You need to hear it." It's only the harsh tone of my voice that has her turning to look at me.

Her face is even paler than it was when I first saw her earlier, her eyes redder and now bloodshot from the tears she's shed. Guilt clenches my stomach that I've had a hand in her pain.

"You lost any right you might have had to tell me what to do the moment you decided to walk out of my life." She pushes away from Erica's desk and steps a little closer to me. My body reacts to her as it always does when we're in touching distance.

"That's just it though, Lauren. The only place I wanted to be that night was in bed with you. The only thing I've ever wanted is you."

"You had me, Ben. I gave you everything and you just stomped all over it."

"I didn't have any other choice."

"It's been six years. I don't care." She waves her hand in front of me and goes to turn away.

Reaching out, I grab her hand and pull her back so she's facing me. Staring down into her eyes, I prepare to say the words that are going to throw her world into a tailspin once again.

"He made me go, Lauren. He threatened your future, your happiness. Both of those things are more important to me than what I wanted."

"Oh that's rich, even for you," she says with a bitter laugh. "I thought it was a huge coincidence that you only showed your face after Dad died, but this is proof that you really were just waiting for him to die to take over."

"I've been waiting for him to rot in hell for a long time, Lauren, trust me." Even her shocked gasp isn't enough for me to regret the words I probably shouldn't have said. But they're true. "He didn't stay away on a golf weekend. He came back. He was waiting for me. Waiting for me to make me leave you."

"You're lying." Wrapping her arms around herself, her body's visibly shaking as she tries to reject the words I'm saying to her.

"I wish. I wish he'd have just accepted how I felt —how I feel—about you. I wish he'd allowed you the happiness you deserve, but just like every other part of his life, he waded in and took control of the situation. It's no different to what he's done here."

"Okay...say everything you're telling me is true. Then why the fuck would he leave this place and the house to you? You're trying to tell me that he hated you to the point that he made you walk out of my life, yet you're the only one listed in his will. What the fuck, Ben?"

She paces up and down in front of me, her fists clenching and unclenching as she tries to process and make sense of what I'm telling her.

"There's nothing here, Lauren. The business is on the verge of going under."

"Bullshit. I do the accounts, the profits are better than they've ever been."

"That's what he makes you believe," Erica says, chipping in for the first time.

"What? You're in on this too?"

"Lauren, trust me when I tell you that I understand how hard all of this is to swallow, but your dad wasn't the kind of man you thought he was."

Lauren looks between the two of us like we've just slapped her. "I don't know what to think. I see all the figures. I see exactly—"

"What he wants you to see."

"How? And why are you only telling me this now?"

"You might want to sit down," Erica says, gesturing to the chair behind Lauren.

"I'm fine. Just tell me what's going on."

"Okay, well...you know how things were for me after Matt and I split up?" Lauren's brows draw together in confusion, but she doesn't interrupt. "Nick knew I was in trouble financially, and he knew I'd do just about anything not to lose my home. So..."

"So?"

"Fucking hell, Lauren." Erica drops her head into her hands and blows out a few slow breaths. "Just remember that I was in a really bad place, okay? He started being really nice, helping me out, giving me lifts home after I sold my car, just little things. He helped me out financially so I wouldn't miss a mortgage payment."

"Right..."

"I slept with him."

"What?" As if Erica's words are like a physical blow to her chest, Lauren stumbles back and crashes into a chair. "Fucking hell. This is a joke, right? This isn't fucking happening," Lauren fumes, walking to the other end of the office. "You slept with my fucking dad?"

"I know how bad this sounds, Lauren. Believe me, none of this was by choice."

"I'm hearing that word a lot today." The laugh that falls from her lips is anything but amused.

"He blackmailed me, Lauren. He made me fall for his charms. He made me need him, and then he made me do exactly what he wanted for fear of the truth coming out and losing my home."

"And what did he make you do? Other than...the obvious." Lauren shivers at the thought while Erica looks like she could puke any second.

"He had me doctoring the figures. Intercepting documents after you'd filed them. Ben's right, there's nothing here. I'm so sorry, Lauren."

"Why the hell didn't you say anything?"

"I couldn't. I was—I *am*—humiliated that I allowed it to happen, but I was drowning and he gave me an out."

"So what you're both trying to tell me is that he made you leave," she says, looking at me, "and he made you sleep with him and cook the books?"

"Jesus, I'm so sorry, Lauren," Erica repeats, but Lauren's already turned away from her.

"This is all your fault. All of it." Her fists slam

down on my chest, but I'm faster than her and I capture her wrists. "If you hadn't let him manipulate you. If you hadn't left. If you'd just fought for what you wanted; none of this would have happened. *That* is your fault," she says, pointing back at Erica, who's wiping away the tears on her cheeks. "All. Of. This. Is. Your. Fault," she says as she fights against her restraints. "And I fucking hate you," she screams. The shock has me releasing her arms, and she runs before I get a chance to stop her.

CHAPTER TWELVE

"WELL, THAT WENT WELL," Erica manages through her tears.

"Fucking hell," I shout, rubbing my hands over my head and down my face. "Now what?"

"Do what you should have done six years ago. Fight for her, Ben."

"What about you?"

"I'm a big girl."

Pulling her into my arms, I drop a kiss to the top of her head. "I'm so sorry you got dragged into this."

"It's my fault. I should have stopped it before it started."

"You weren't to know he was using you."

"Maybe not, but I knew nothing good could come of it. I need to talk to Jenny."

"I think that's a good idea."

"Really?" she asks, pulling back so she can look at me.

"Yeah. If we've got any hope of keeping any of this, we all need to be on the same page. No more lies. No more deception and bullshit."

"I couldn't agree more. She's going to hate me."

"I think she'll be more understanding than you expect. After all, how do you think he managed to worm his way in here in the first place?"

"Motherfucker."

I was only a kid when they got together. I have no idea how it all happened and what Nick's intentions were. They could have been totally honourable and he could have loved her, but knowing him now, I highly doubt it.

"I need to find Lauren."

"She said she was meant to be seeing Danni this afternoon. She's probably gone there."

"Where's there?" After getting the address, I go to leave but stop at the main door to the office. "Erica?"

"Yeah?"

"Why are you here on a Sunday?"

"Someone's got to try to keep this place from going under."

"Has anyone told you that you're a little bit awesome?"

"Yeah, every now and then." She tries to make it sound light, but I hear the sadness in her tone. Somehow, I think every now and then might be pushing it.

"Well, you are. I'll be back to help, promise."

"Just go and get your girl, Ben."

"SHE'S NOT FUCKING HERE. How many times?" Danni asks, standing her ground at her front door.

"You're lying."

"I'd do anything for Lauren. I'd lie for her time and again if I needed to, but seriously, she's not here." Not buying her excuses, I barge past her. "Come in, why don't you?"

I find two people sitting on her sofa, but other than that her flat is empty and my stomach drops.

"Happy now?" Danni asks when I join her and her friends back in the living room.

"I'm sorry," I mutter, regretfully.

"What's happened?"

"She's finally learnt the truth."

"What? That you're a weak fucking pussy?"

"Whoa. Who's bent your knickers out of shape?"

"None of your fucking business. Just like Lauren is none of yours. You need to stay away from her. You've already done enough damage."

"Whatever. Do you have any idea where she is?" Her eyebrows rise and she defiantly puts her hands on her hips. "Okay, well...it was nice seeing you."

I let myself out of her fancy basement flat and find my car where I left it half parked on the kerb, thankfully without a ticket.

Resting back, I wonder what I should do now, but the only thing I can see is the dejected look on Lauren's face as she walked away from me. I know she probably doesn't want me chasing her down right now, but we just dropped two huge bombs on her. I need to know she's okay.

Fighting my need to go back to the office and find her address, I drive to my favourite place. By the time I'm pulling up to the deserted car park that overlooks the city below, the sun is starting to set. Soft orange hues make the hustle and bustle in the distance look almost inviting. This place is the escape from reality that I need.

Disappointment hits me when I turn the corner

and spot another car at the far end—that is, until I take it in properly.

She's here.

Pulling up next to her car, I look inside and find it empty. Where the fuck is she?

Quickly getting out without shutting off the engine, the music continues playing behind me as I go in search of the woman who still holds my heart in my hands.

The moment I walk to the edge of the car park, I see her. She's laid out on a blanket on the grass bank.

Walking over, I drop down beside her and stare at her peaceful face. Her eyelashes are resting down on her tear-stained cheeks. Her lips are slightly parted as she blows out shallow breaths.

She's so fucking beautiful, my heart aches for her.

"I'm so sorry, Lauren," I whisper. She can't hear me, but the need to say it gets the better of me.

Reaching forward, I brush a loose strand of hair from her face, but I'm not gentle enough.

Her eyes fly open as she scrambles to sit up. "Jesus fucking Christ, Ben."

"Sorry, I didn't mean to scare you. You shouldn't fall asleep out here. Anything could happen to you."

"Like being scared to death by you?"

"I'm the last person you should be scared of."

"I'm not so sure about that." Everything that's happened in the last few days seems to hit her all at once because her soft, sleepy eyes suddenly turn hard. She looks away from me, cutting herself off.

"Lauren, please don't do that. Can we just talk?"

"Talk? What would you like to talk about exactly? How you broke my heart? About how my dad apparently was intent on ruining my life along with everyone else's that I care about? About how you promised to protect me and you just fucking left?"

I pause and stare at her for a few seconds. After imagining her for so long, being able to sit beside her, to breathe the same air as her, feels surreal.

When I don't respond, she turns her blue eyes on me.

"The weather?" I ask, remembering that she asked me a question.

The skin around her eyes crinkles before the most amazing sound fills my ears. Laughter.

I can't help but laugh along with her as she lets out some of the tension she's been carrying around with her.

She laughs for the longest time. I really hope it helps her as much as it does me. Once she's calmed down, she looks up at me and smiles. "Thanks. I needed that."

"Glad I could help."

"It doesn't fix anything though."

Reaching out, I tuck the same stray piece of hair back behind her ear. "Doesn't it?"

Slapping my arm away, she puts a little more distance between us. "Why do you keep doing this?"

"Doing what?"

"Acting like nothing's changed. It's been six years, Ben. Everything's changed. I've changed. What I want has changed."

"Has it? Because from where I'm sitting, you still have the same passion and desire in your eyes as you did back then. Your body reacts in exactly the same way. You're just too scared to admit that nothing's really changed at all." Closing the space between us, I whisper, "Not where we're concerned."

"Stop it. I've moved on."

"See, there you go again. Pretending that's true."

"It is true. You've met him." She can't hold my eyes as she says this and turns to look over the city.

"Hmm...so I have. Look at me and tell me you love him. That you love him like you did me."

Anger fills her eyes when she looks back. "How dare you ask me that?"

"What? It's a simple question. Do you love him?"

"Of course."

"Like you did me?"

Her silence says everything I need to hear.

"No, I didn't think so."

"I'm leaving." Lauren jumps up from the blanket and goes to march towards her car. Unfortunately for her, I'm faster.

"No, you're not." Wrapping my arm around her waist, I pull her back until she's pressed up against my chest.

"Tell me you don't fall asleep at night wishing it was me next to you. Tell me it's not me you imagine when he's getting you off."

"He doesn't—" She slams her lips together to stop herself saying more. Her reaction soothes the sting of even suggesting another man might have touched her. "No, Ben. No."

"You're lying."

Our eye contact holds, our breaths mingling, our chests heaving. As much as I want to make the first move, as desperate as I am to feel her soft lips against mine, I know I need to wait for her to do it.

"Fuck you, Ben. Fuck you." Lifting up, her lips press against mine.

I wait a second for her to regret it, but when she doesn't pull back, I make the move I'm desperate for.

My fingers slide into her hair, while my other arm continues to hold her around the waist and I lower her back down onto the blanket.

Sliding my hand over her neck, I find the zip on the front of her hoodie and pull it down. We both know who it belongs to, and it needs to go. The second it's undone, I find the hem of her top and slip my hand underneath. I need more of her. I need to feel her soft skin against mine.

"Fuck, Ben. We can't—"

"Shhh." Kissing down the sensitive skin of her neck, I lick across her collarbone and pull the fabric of her vest down to reveal her full breast.

"We're out in the open."

"I've never seen anyone else here. It's safe. Take a risk with me, Lauren." I flick my eyes up to hers and they're met with burning passion. There's no way she's stopping this right now.

Pulling the cup of her bra down, I suck her puckered nipple into my mouth.

"Fuuuck, Ben," she moans, arching to give me more.

"I fucking love it when you're desperate for me."

"I'm always desperate for you." The second she

registers that she said the words aloud, she sucks in a breath and bites down on her bottom lip.

"I know. I can see it every time you look at me. It's like you're begging me to find out just how badly you need me." Popping the button on her jeans, I slip my hand inside and beneath the lace covering her. "You're soaked for me, aren't you?"

She doesn't respond, so I dip my head and bite down on her exposed nipple.

"All you can think about is how I'll feel inside you again, isn't it?"

I don't get a chance to take her in my mouth again because she nods. "Yes, yes. Please."

Satisfied that she's admitting what she really wants, I slide my fingers lower and find her exactly as I was expecting.

"Fucking hell, Lauren." Taking her lips again, I tease her clit and dip my fingers inside her just enough to drive her fucking crazy with need.

I kiss her until I'm breathless and she's writhing beneath me, desperate for more.

Pulling my hand from her jeans, I sit her up and pull her hoodie, vest, and bra off. I need more. Squeezing both her breasts in my hands, she moans and bucks her hips against me. My cock presses against the fly of my jeans, desperate to be released.

Pulling her trainers from her feet, I slide her jeans and knickers down her legs.

Reaching back, I pull my t-shirt over my head. Her eyes immediately drop to my exposed skin and she runs her tongue along her bottom lip.

"It's yours whenever you like. You just gotta say the word, Lauren."

Her eyes focus a little more, and I worry that I just said the wrong thing, but instead of shying away, she reaches out for my fly.

Her delicate fingers make light work of undoing the button and zip and parting the fabric. Running her hands around the sensitive skin under my waistband, she slides them into the back of my jeans and grabs onto my arse. Her nails dig into my skin and I find her lips, pulling her bottom one into my mouth and biting down until I hear her soft gasp of surprise.

Forcing the fabric down my thighs, my cock springs free. She rips her lips away from mine and looks down. My cock twitches under her stare. I'm lost in my imagination for what's coming next, so I'm caught totally off-guard as she shoves my shoulders and I fall backwards onto the blanket ungracefully. Lauren wastes no time. Throwing her leg over my waist, she lines herself up exactly where I need her.

She grinds down on my cock and a growl rumbles up my throat.

"This is fucking everything," I manage to get out as she takes me in her hand and slowly lowers herself.

"Fuck." She throws her head back as the sensation washes through her.

She comes to a stop when she's fully seated, but it's not enough for me. Grabbing onto her hips, I lift her and then slam her back down.

I hit her so deep that her head flies forward and her shocked eyes find mine.

"Just reminding you who you belong to, baby."

"Fuck you." It comes out as a gasp as I slam up into her once again. Her walls ripple around me; she's already close to finding her release.

Needing to feel her clamping down on me, I release one of her hips in favour of teasing her clit.

"Fuck, Ben," she moans, grinding her hips against me.

"Come, Lauren. Remind yourself what it's like, because you know as well as I do that no one else makes you feel this good."

"Fucking. Hate. You," she shouts, her body tensing as her orgasm claims her. Every muscle in her body convulses with the pleasure that races through her. I continue thrusting up into her and allow her to ride out every second of her release.

Drained of energy, she falls onto my chest.

"This is how it's meant to be, Lauren."

Unable to find her voice, she instead sinks her teeth into my pec. The sensation shoots straight to my cock and I explode on a roar, emptying everything I have inside her.

Once my body's come down from its high, I shift us and roll Lauren onto her back. If she believes I'm done with her for tonight, she's going to have a shock.

I settle myself between her thighs and take her lips in a wet and dirty kiss.

"I don't know how it's possible, but we're even more explosive than we were back then, baby."

Her nails scratch down my back as I suck one of her nipples into my mouth and release it with a pop.

The lyrics of Avicii and Rita Ora's *Lonely Together* float around the otherwise silent night around us, and I can't help thinking that it's perfect for right now.

I pepper kisses down her stomach, pausing when I hit her belly button. Looking up, I find her watching my every move.

The words start falling from my lips before I've

realised. I can't help myself. "Lauren, I never stopped lo—"

"Don't." No sooner has she barked the word than she's scrambling out from beneath me and snatching up her discarded clothes.

"No, stop." I try grabbing at the fabric of her jeans as she shoves her leg in, but she manages to pull it from my grasp. Standing, I pull my own jeans up and watch as she quickly puts on the rest of her clothes.

"Enough, Ben. This was a mistake."

"No, it really wasn't. This was meant to happen. *We* are meant to happen, Lauren."

"No, we're not."

She may as well have just stabbed a knife through my heart.

"How can you say that?" My voice sounds just as defeated as I feel. I take a step towards her, but she takes two back.

"All of this was a mistake. I never should have gone anywhere near you. It was wrong, and we both knew it."

"There's nothing wrong with how I feel about you." I try reaching for her again, but she's backing up too quickly.

"You ruined my life, Ben. This is done. *We* are done."

I fight to breathe as she turns and runs towards her car.

"Lauren," I cry as her tyres kick up the stones covering the car park. But it's too late.

She's gone.

CHAPTER THIRTEEN

ONCE THE SOUND of her engine disappears, I fall back down on the blanket. At some point over the last hour or so, night descended around us and the only light is coming from the moon that's shining brightly above me.

I stare up at the star-filled sky as emotion clogs my throat and stings my eyes.

I tell myself that she didn't mean any of those words. She can't. I can see how she really feels when we're together. It's no different to our first few times all those years ago. I know it's not just me who still feels the connection between us. Hell, she's fucked me twice in the past week. There's definitely still something between us. There has to be.

Lauren's the only girl ever to own my heart, and

I'm not letting her go because she's too stubborn to admit what we could be. I know I hurt her. I feel the guilt and pain of that day every waking moment. She's not the only one who had her heart broken.

The night chill eventually gets to me and I find myself back in my car. Rita's still singing away, but even her voice doesn't have the effect it usually does.

Not feeling strong enough to return to the house where so much has happened with Lauren, I head back to the office.

This time, all the lights are off and the place is deserted. I walk through the darkness until I'm in what was once my dad's office. I flick the desk lamp on and power up the computer.

I'm determined to give this business the lease of life it needs to stop it from going under, and in order for that to happen I need to start getting my head around what's going on.

I get so lost in everything that before I know it, the sun's starting to come up and the sound of someone entering drags my eyes up from the screen.

"Have you been here all night?" Erica correctly guesses when she finds me probably looking a little worse for wear.

"Looks that way."

"Are you okay? You seem…"

"I'm fine. Just trying to get my head around everything."

"Did you find Lauren yesterday?" I make a noise in agreement and Erica's eyebrow pops up in question. "I'll go make coffee and you can tell me all about it."

"Nothing to tell." The pain I felt as she drove away from me last night once again tugs at my heart.

"Try telling your face that."

I manage to distract Erica with a million work-related questions when she reappears thankfully with a steaming mug of coffee. I know she hasn't forgotten though. I can see it in the sympathetic looks I get while she thinks I'm doing something else. I know she wants to help, but quite honestly, I've no idea if anyone can do anything to help right now. Lauren made her thoughts very clear last night. I now just need to decide what I'm going to do about it.

Once the others start arriving for the day, Erica leaves me to it. I need to go home and get some sleep really, but now I've started getting to grips with this place once again, I'm desperate to continue. This might be the only thing I have here now, so I've no choice but to make a success of it.

I'm looking over a set of drawings when someone knocks on the office door.

"Come in," I call without looking up, because I assume it's either Erica or Betty with more coffee.

"We need to talk," an unfamiliar male voice says, dragging my eyes up from the desk.

"What the—" He might look like a different person from the first time I met him, but I know immediately that the man standing in front of me is Joe. *The boyfriend.* But this time, there's no crisp white shirt, braces, or slicked-back hair. Instead, he's wearing a skin-tight black t-shirt, two solid arms full of tattoos on display, and a Johnson & Son's high visibility jacket. "You've got to be shitting me."

Closing the door behind him, cutting off any prying eyes, he walks over to my desk and places his palms down. If he's trying to intimidate me with his muscles and ink, it's failing miserably.

My muscles twitch to stand toe-to-toe with him but I resist, not wanting to look like he affects me in any way. Instead, I rest back in my chair and plaster a neutral expression on my face.

"You need to stay away from her."

"Not happening. Did you need anything else?" Fire flicks through his eyes and I just about manage to contain my smile. Going a round or two with this guy might be the exact thing I need to ease the tension coursing through me, but I want it to be a challenge. When I beat him, I want it to be known that it's because I'm the better man.

"Do you have any idea what you're doing to her?"

"I know exactly what I did to her last night," I taunt. His jaw pops and the muscles in his neck tense. "Didn't she tell you?"

"Of course she fucking told me. Lauren's not a liar." My eyes widen slightly at his admission. "I know everything, Ben. I know every bit of pain you've caused her. I also know that it's time for you to disappear off to wherever it was you went before and to leave her the fuck alone."

"Make me," I state, deciding now's the perfect time to properly get in his face. There's about an inch between us when the door swings open and Lauren rushes in.

"For fuck's sake." She grabs Joe's arm and attempts to pull him away. "I told you to leave it."

"This needs fucking sorting, sweets."

Sweets? Who the fuck does this guy think he is?

"Just get your arse to site like you promised you would." Lauren's anger is palpable, and it makes me weirdly happy to know that it's not directed at me for once.

"If he so much as touches you again, I'll fucking kill him," Joe seethes.

"He won't." Lauren's words seem a little too confident for my liking. I know for a fact that if I got her in the right situation, she'd be like putty in my hands once again. The spark between us is too strong for her to deny, and she knows it just as well as I do. It's about time that this fucker realised it as well and got out of my fucking way.

"I'm serious," he says, turning his dark stare on me. A weaker man might cower to him, but that's not who I am. Standing taller, I tip my chin up to him. "You fucking touch her—"

"*And you'll kill me.* Yeah, I got that memo thanks. Are we done here? I've got a business to run, and I'm sure you've got some bricks to move or something."

"Actually, Joe's one of our site agents," Lauren says. "You might want to start being nice to him."

"Get out of my office," I growl. I've not had enough sleep or caffeine to deal with this right now.

"I'm fucking watching you," Joe warns.

"I'm real scared," I mutter as he turns and walks away. I don't see his reaction because my eyes are locked on Lauren as she tries to contain a smile.

"You need to start fighting your own battles, baby. You don't need a henchman to do it for you."

"You and I both know what happens when we fight. I think it's best we stay out of each other's way. I'll be working from home if anyone needs me." Spinning on her heel, she walks out of the office and, after a very brief chat with Erica, she leaves the building.

"YOU SLEPT WITH HER AGAIN, didn't you?"

"Sorry, I'm working," I say over my shoulder, feeling Erica's eyes burning into the back of my head.

"You need to stop playing games, Ben."

Spinning on my chair, I find her with her hands on her hips, staring daggers at me.

"What?"

"Lauren's one of my best friends, and you're hurting her. You need to stop."

"I thought I was your friend?"

"You are. But you're the one doing all of this. Just do as she asks and leave her be. She's moved on with her life, and you need to do the same."

"You're serious?"

"I want nothing more than for both of you to be happy, but at the moment you're ripping each other apart."

"We're meant to be together."

"Maybe so, but not right now. Just give her some time. Give her some space to breathe."

"So he can get his claws in even deeper?"

"Just trust her, Ben. Trust that she knows what she's doing."

"How can I when she's been sleeping with me?"

ERICA EVENTUALLY LEAVES THE OFFICE, but I only get a few minutes of peace before four others descend on me.

"Here he is!" Dec announces as he swings the door open. "Shit, you look rough, mate."

"Nice to see you, too."

"We've been waiting at the house for you. We need to head back home."

Guilt washes through me that I've basically abandoned them after they came all this way to try to cheer me up. "Shit, guys. I'm—"

"Don't even think about it. We came here to support you, not to make you feel guilty for doing your thing," Liv says, giving me a stern look.

I smile at her, but I don't feel any better about any of this. "This place is about to go under, and my darling stepdaddy left it all to me."

"Yeah, your mum mentioned something along those lines. Is there anything we can do?" Dec asks.

"Got a few hundred grand to spare?" Dec looks a little too serious. "I'm joking, I'm joking. I'm sure it'll all be fine once I get back into the swing of it."

"Well, you know where we are if there is anything."

"I hate leaving you like this," Liv whispers in my ear when I pull her in for a hug.

"I'll be fine. You don't need to worry about me."

"Keep me informed about everything."

"I will."

Saying goodbye to the people who've basically been my family for the past few years is more emotional than I expected it to be. When I left Devon, I wasn't expecting my life there to come to an end, but looking at how things have turned out here, it seems that might just be the case.

Walking back into the office once they've left, I'm met with a sea of concerned faces, and it reminds me that I haven't slept.

"Are you going to be okay holding the fort?" I ask Erica when I come to a stop by her desk.

"Of course. Who do you think's been running this place for the last two weeks?"

"I'll never be able to thank you enough."

"Ben, I caused half of this. It's my job to try to help put it right. I'm just grateful I still have a job."

"Don't be stupid. You're not going anywhere. Call if you need me, but there's a good chance I'll be sleeping."

"I've got it covered. Go look after yourself."

Laughter fills the house when I get home. Poking my head into the living room, I find Mum and Chris laughing at something on the TV. I can't help but smile at them both. Maybe what everyone has been saying is true, and things will all be okay in the end. An image of Lauren pops into my head, but I push it to the back of my mind—for now, at least. I just need to be happy that Mum's able to move past the disaster that was her late husband and the legacy he's left behind.

Memories of my time with Lauren last night fill my mind as I shower. The scent of her perfume has lingered around me since the moment she left. I'm not all that happy about washing it away.

My body's just about ready to crash when I drag my feet towards my bed. Crawling under the covers, I fall asleep the second my head hits the pillow.

CHAPTER FOURTEEN

I WAKE with a start and one thought running through my mind.

Joe knows we slept together, yet he didn't take my head off.

I don't stop to question my decision. Instead, I jump out of bed and drag on some fresh clothes.

"Ben?" Mum calls from the kitchen as I race towards the front door. "Is everything okay?"

"Yeah. What's Lauren's address?"

"I can't...I promised..."

"Don't worry. I'll find it."

"What are you doing?"

"Going to claim what's mine." Pride fills her face, but I don't miss the slight concern that's also present.

It makes my determination to get this sorted right now falter slightly.

"Are you sure this is a good idea? She's already been through so much."

"I need her, Mum. I can't sit around and watch her with someone else when she's shown that she needs me too."

"You just need to give her time, Ben. She'll figure it all out when she's ready. You pushing her into it isn't going to help."

That doubt niggles at me again, but my need for her is stronger. "I can't stand by and watch her make a huge mistake with him. I won't do it. Wish me luck," I say, reaching for the door handle and pulling it open.

"Good luck," she calls out, but I'm already getting in my car.

The drive to the office takes longer than I think it ever has before, but the second I pull up, I race through to my office and power up the computer. Finding the folder full of all our employees' personal details, I find Lauren's and note down her address.

I don't bother taking the time to shut it back down again. I'm too intent on finding her and sorting this out once and for all.

She lives farther out of the city than I was

expecting. I manage to get stuck at every set of traffic lights on the way, but before long, I'm jogging up the stairs towards the flat listed as hers and Joe's after a young mum with a little boy helpfully held the main door open for me.

Knocking on the door, I hear movement inside the flat. My heart thunders in my chest as I impatiently wait for it to open.

Finally, there's a click, and a slither of light from inside shines around the wooden door. But when it's pulled back enough to see the person at the other side, what I find isn't what I was expecting. Lauren's standing there, and her hair's a mess, sticking up in all directions. She's just wearing a man's t-shirt.

Her eyes harden as she watches me take in her appearance. "What are you doing here?" She's slightly out of breath, and it only ignites my anger.

"Who is it, sweets?" a male voice rumbles, before the door opens even wider to reveal Joe coming to a stop behind her in just his boxers. "Oh, it's you," he spits, sliding his arm around Lauren's waist and pulling her to him before dropping his lips to her exposed neck.

Something inside me explodes. My nostrils flare and my teeth grind as I try to keep myself from ripping his fucking limbs from his body.

"Did you want something?" he asks while Lauren stands stock still in his arms.

"I came for what's mine."

"Nothing here is yours, mate."

"Don't fucking ma—"

"He's right," Lauren says. Her eyes find mine, and I see a determination in them that wasn't there moments ago. "There's nothing here for you anymore."

"But—"

"There are no buts, Ben. I told you last night. I'm done. This is over. Stay if you want, for your business, but I won't be there. You'll find my resignation in your Inbox already. I. Am. Done."

"I'm proud of you, sweets," Joe whispers in her ear, holding her tight.

A lump the size of a fucking basketball climbs up my throat. I have no choice but to turn and walk away. I'd give everything to Lauren, but she won't see my tears.

Ben and Lauren's story concludes in *Fighting for the Forbidden*. PRE-ORDER NOW

ACKNOWLEDGMENTS

Writing this part of Lauren and Ben's story just about broke me. It was hard going and so incredibly emotional, but the heartache had to happen.

I'm not desperate to dive straight into the third and final part of their story to attempt to soothe their broken hearts and to find out a little more about what happened in the long six years they were apart. But don't worry, I'm not going to make it easy for them. There's still plenty of anger and betrayal to come.

Once again, I need to say a HUGE thank you to my alpha reader, Michelle. You've been there with me word for word, egging me on and listening to me talk myself in circles over how all of this was going to play out. Oh, and of course you were the one who demanded that I break Ben and make him cry. I hope you're happy with yourself!

My beta team, Deanna, Helen, Lindsay, Suzanne and Tracy. Thank you so much for dropping everything to find out more about Lauren and Ben, and for now being too mean when I left you hanging once again with no date for a follow up. Your feedback as always is priceless and all your words and theories are still spinning in my mind as I plan book three.

Evelyn, once again thank you so much for working your magic and making my words as pretty as they can be. I seriously couldn't do this without you.

And as always, last but never least, my husband and daughter for supporting me and allowing me to follow this crazy dream.

Until next time,

Tracy xo

ABOUT THE AUTHOR

Tracy Lorraine is a M/F and M/M contemporary romance author. Tracy has just turned thirty and lives in a cute Cotswold village in England with her husband, baby girl and lovable but slightly crazy dog. Having always been a bookaholic with her head stuck in her Kindle, Tracy decided to try her hand at a story idea she dreamt up and hasn't looked back since.

Be the first to find out about new releases and offers. Sign up to my newsletter here.

If you want to know what I'm up to and see teasers and snippets of what I'm working on, then you need to be in my Facebook group. Join Tracy's Angels here.

Keep up to date with Tracy's books at
www.tracylorraine.com

ALSO BY TRACY LORRAINE

Falling Series

Falling for Ryan: Part One #1

Falling for Ryan: Part Two #2

Falling for Jax #3

Falling for Daniel (An Falling Series Novella)

Falling for Ruben #4

Falling for Fin #5

Falling for Lucas #6

Falling for Caleb #7

Falling for Declan #8

Falling For Liam #9

Forbidden Series

Falling for the Forbidden

Losing the Forbidden

Fighting for the Forbidden

Ruined Series

Ruined Plans #1

Ruined by Lies #2

Ruined Promises #3

Never Forget Series

Never Forget Him #1

Never Forget Us #2

Everywhere & Nowhere #3

Chasing Series

Chasing Logan

The Cocktail Girls

His Manhattan

Her Kensington

Flirt Club

His Sorority Sweetheart

Cheeky Trifle

Santa's Naughty Elf

Resolution: Exposure

Dear All Star Player

Forever Ruined (A Ruined series spin off)

Mr. Silver

Spring Break Secret Baby

His Cherry Blossom

Something Borrowed

Her Smokin' Firefighter

SNEAK PEEK

Falling for the Forbidden is a spin off from my *Falling* series. If you've not read it then keep reading for a sneak peek at *Falling for Ryan*, my friends to lovers romance that kicks off the series.

FALLING FOR RYAN: PART ONE

Molly

Eight years ago...

"MUM, I'm going to Becky's sixteenth birthday party tonight, then sleeping at Hannah's," I remind her as I walk into the kitchen where she's sat with her head in an interior design magazine, waving her hands around—presumably trying to dry her nail varnish. I pull out a can of Coke from the fridge before continuing. "I've taken the litre bottle of vodka from the drinks cabinet, and I've got a pack of condoms...

you know, just in case." I lean back against the counter and watch for a reaction. *Any* reaction.

"Uh huh."

"I'm pretty sure some of the boys are bringing ecstasy."

"Hmm..." She hums as she turns a page and studies the room pictured.

"Didn't you only have a manicure yesterday? Why are you painting your nails already?"

Now, that gets her attention. Her head snaps up the moment the words 'nails' and 'manicure' leave my mouth. Surprise, surprise; my mother cares more about that than about alcohol, drugs, sex...and me.

"Yes, I did, but I just couldn't find a thing to wear tonight."

I doubt that's actually true, seeing as she's recently turned my eldest brother's old room into her personal wardrobe after already filling her own walk-in. "So, I went to that little boutique in town this morning and found the most perfect dress. Your dad will love it, but it didn't match the colour I chose for my nails yesterday."

"Wow, what a disaster," I mutter as I leave the room. "I'll be going out in about an hour. *Not that you really care.*" I say the last bit quieter, but I'm not sure why; when I look back, Mum is once again too engrossed in her magazine to acknowledge me.

I let out a huge breath and head back up to my room to finish packing for the party. I'm getting ready with my best friend Hannah and her twin Emma, who live next door. We've all been friends for as long as I can remember. Being twins, Hannah and Emma are really close, but Hannah and I are not far behind. The three of us do almost everything together; their parents have often joked that they have triplets, really.

I always laugh along.

Even though they know what my life is like, I don't think any of them really appreciate how much I wish that were true.

I'm just shoving my fourth outfit choice for the night into my bag when I hear my brother downstairs, greeting Mum. She instantly responds to him, which makes me laugh to myself, although it's anything but funny. One of her golden boys has come to visit. I bet if he needed something, she'd ruin that new nail varnish in an instant. God, I can't wait to get out of this hellhole I call home.

"Is Molly still here?" Daniel asks.

Her reply sounds suspiciously like, "I have no idea."

Walking to the other side of the room, I rest my hands on the windowsill and blow out a long breath as I gaze out over the countryside, trying to calm myself down. I keep telling myself not to get worked up by their actions, but sometimes it's easier said than done.

"Hey sis, I'm glad you're still here," Daniel says as he enters my room a few minutes later. My brothers are a lot older than me; I was an unplanned accident fifteen and a half years ago. Daniel is my youngest older brother and, at thirty years old, he's crazy protective of me. Steven is, too, but he now has a serious girlfriend so I'm seeing less of him these days. Daniel is my idol—always has been. He doesn't take life too seriously, does exactly as he pleases, works bloody hard, but always has fun. That's exactly what I want my life to be like, and I plan on making it so—once I get out on my own.

"Hey." I only manage one word because, as soon as I see him, I burst into tears. He pulls me into a tight hug. I hate that Mum and Dad can do this to me. Can make me feel so worthless. It makes me angry every time a tear falls for their actions. I wish I could be stronger.

"What have they done now?" Daniel asks. Both

he and Steven know how our parents treat me. Hell, I couldn't count the number of arguments I've overheard about it on both hands and feet, but nothing ever changes. I'm just grateful that I have two amazing older brothers to turn to if I need to. Plus, I have my adopted family next door, who I'm pretty sure would do just about anything for me if I needed it.

"Nothing. I'm fine," I say, pulling away from him and wiping my eyes. I look at him and see the questions in his. "No, really; I'm just being a silly, hormonal teenager."

"Hmm...whatever you say, Molls. You still going to that party tonight?" I don't believe for a second that he buys my lie, but he knows it's easier for me not to discuss it. Nothing he can say is going to make any of it better, anyway.

"Of course, why?"

"I got you something." I watch as he reaches into his coat pocket and pulls out a small bottle of vodka before handing it to me.

"What's this for?" He looks at me and quirks an eyebrow. "I know it's to drink, you fool, but why are you giving it to me?"

"Because I remember what it was like being your

age, and I didn't think anyone else would be buying you some. You deserve to act your age, Molly. Let your hair down. You work too damn hard trying to get your grades. But please be sensible. I don't want to be visiting you in the hospital or be an uncle yet. Actually..." He pauses as he reaches into his back pocket and pulls out his wallet.

My eyes widen in embarrassment. "No, no, no... I'm good, you don't need to worry about that."

I hate to admit it, but Daniel is the only one who knows what I've been up to. He let himself into my room one day while I was in my ensuite to find an open box of condoms on the bed and, being the protective brother that he is, counted them and realised two were missing. I'm hoping he doesn't want more of an explanation than that, because I really don't want to sit here and explain to my adult brother that I took myself off to the doctors a while ago and got myself on the pill—you know, just in case. Wouldn't that make Mummy and Daddy proud, to be grandparents while their daughter was still a teenager? Imagine the embarrassment.

"Okay, well, have a good time tonight, and ring me if you have any problems, yeah?"

"I promise."

I know I mentioned drugs and alcohol to my mum downstairs, but my group of friends isn't really into all that. I only said it as a way to provoke her in the hopes of getting some kind of reaction. Yes, there are plenty of kids at school who are at it every weekend, but my group actually cares about getting good grades and good jobs. The bottle of vodka Daniel just handed me will probably be it for us tonight.

"See you later then, kid," he says before kissing my forehead and leaving my room.

"THAT WAS AWESOME," Hannah squeals as the three of us stumble into the twins' bedroom sometime in the early hours of Sunday morning. Emma heads straight over to her side of the room and immediately starts replacing her party clothes with her pyjamas, while Hannah and I sit on her bed and reflect on the evening.

"So...come on, spill it...where did you go with Callum?" Hannah pleads.

"Just for a walk in the garden. I told you earlier!"

"I didn't believe you then, and I still don't now. I

saw you two getting off with each other in the corner before you disappeared."

Callum is the boy at school that every girl dreams of. He's sporty, clever, funny and, of course, seriously hot, which is exactly why no one expected him to show his face tonight. But he did, and let's just say that I got to know him a little better than I did before. I'm yet to decide if that's a good thing or not.

"Will you two keep it down? I want to get up early tomorrow to do some coursework before we go to Grandma's," Emma complains from her bed.

Okay, so I said before that we work hard to get good grades, but Emma takes it to the extreme. I was actually surprised she gave herself tonight off. She's doing A-level maths already and does Spanish lessons after school to get herself an extra GCSE. I think she's putting too much pressure on herself, but she can't seem to stop in her quest to be the best accountant Oxford has ever seen.

"Sorry," we whisper simultaneously.

"So...come on, Molly, tell me," Hannah says, keeping her voice low.

I let out a frustrated breath and go for it. "Okay, so we went outside and found a quiet corner in the garden behind a bush. He pulled me down to the ground and we kissed for a while and let our hands...

roam a little." I look up at Hannah and can see her excitement about what might come next.

"Oh my God, did you have sex with him?" she asks, but says the word *sex* much quieter. I don't know why; it's only Emma who could be listening.

"No, I didn't. I sorta thought we were going to, but by the time I got into his boxers, he was so worked up that he went off like a firework!" I can't help it, I burst out laughing at the memory, earning me another grumble from Emma.

"But I thought Callum's slept with loads of girls?" Hannah asks, confused.

"That's what the rumour mill says...I would be inclined to say that this was his first experience and the rumours are just that: rumours." We fall about giggling like the schoolgirls we are; I guess that vodka hasn't totally worn off yet.

"So, you *were* going to have sex with him, then?"

"Yeah, I guess," I say, shrugging my shoulders.

"But don't you want to wait until you're in love?" she asks innocently.

The only thing I have never told my best friend is that I lost my virginity last year at a party. Hannah has a different outlook on life thanks to her normal, loving family, and I don't want to have to explain my reasons for doing what I did that night—and a few times since. I totally understand her desire to wait until she's in love, and I admire her for it, but what I needed that night—what I *still* need—is to feel wanted by someone. And that first night? That was exactly how I felt.

FALLING FOR RYAN: PART ONE

CHAPTER ONE

Molly

Present

IT'S MIDNIGHT, and I've been sat on Ryan's doorstep for nearly an hour. I've already started on one of the bottles of wine. Although it was a scorching summer's day, the heat has now worn off, the clouds have gathered, and it's lumping it down with rain. I'm trying to tuck myself into his little porch to stop from getting so wet, but with the wind direction, it's not doing much good. I'm soaked through. It was a silly idea to pick white t-shirts when

I rebranded the coffee shop; thank God for padded bras!

By the time I'd cleaned and locked up, it was just gone ten. I love working at Cocoa's and have done so since I was sixteen. Hannah and Emma's parents own it. Susan started the business after she finished university. She came into some inheritance and, with the money, Cocoa's was born. The place was a huge part of my childhood. Hannah, Emma, and I would go there after school to do homework or just chat about boys, and it pretty much stayed that way until we finished university. We still have a booth in the back corner dedicated to us.

I will forever be grateful for Susan and her husband, Pete, whom she actually met as a customer in Cocoa's. It was love at first sight for them. Not only did they give me a job, but they took me under their wing when I was much younger.

Megan, who works in the evenings, had a phone call from her boyfriend at eight o'clock saying their little boy was really sick. I let her go home to be with him and finished up the rest of the night on my own.

Once I got in my car, all I could think about was having a nice hot bath and snuggling into bed in my tiny one-bed flat with my boyfriend, Max. We've been together on and off for the past three years, but when Hannah, whom I'd lived with above the coffee shop, decided eight months ago that she wanted her own boyfriend to move into the flat, I decided it was time I moved out and left them to it. Max had suggested I move in with him. I wasn't thrilled by the idea, to be honest, but at the time I didn't have the money to find anywhere decent to live. I hate being alone. I would have had to find someone who was renting out a room anyway, so it seemed like a sensible suggestion and a logical step in our relationship.

A week later, we all moved. Me into Max's flat, and Hannah's boyfriend into the one we'd shared for the past six years.

The ten-minute drive to our home seemed to take forever. I pulled up out the front; it was weird to be parking next to Max's car. He had worked nights the whole time I'd known him.

I dragged my body up the stairs to the third floor and let myself in. I shut the door behind me; the only light was coming from the bedroom. My heart dropped into my stomach when I heard voices and strange noises coming from down the hallway. As quietly as I could, I tiptoed towards them.

When I got to the door, I couldn't believe my eyes. Now, I knew Max was no angel, but I was under the impression that we had put the past behind us when we decided to live together and had become a monogamous couple. Yes, the past few months had been a strain, but still.

What was happening before my eyes on our bed showed me how wrong I was.

I numbly slipped back down the hallway and grabbed a couple of pairs of knickers that, luckily for me, were drying on the radiator, and left.

I tried to keep myself together as I made a pit stop at the shop on my way to Ryan's house. I didn't want to be one of those emotional women sobbing in the alcohol aisle, trying to decide which bottle would make me forget.

Once I'd paid for two bottles of my favourite wine and a crate of lager for Ryan, I made my way over to his new house. He'd only moved in two weeks ago, although it was months ago that he made the decision to buy the three-story townhouse in the new development on the outskirts of the city. It was basically a pile of bricks when he took me with him to see it for the first time, but I could see why he'd fallen in love with it. It was modern and spacious, with amazing views across fields from the back. From the front, you could see all the lights from the city in the distance. Because it was yet to be finished, it meant Ryan could choose a lot of the interior to suit his taste, and he didn't have to spend his whole summer re-decorating.

Grabbing my phone, I open up my messages to re-read the conversation I'd had with him earlier. He said he was going out tonight to celebrate the end of the school year but that he wasn't expecting to be home late. I guess that didn't really go as planned—not that he'd be expecting me to be sitting here waiting for him.

I'm starting to think I should have gone somewhere else. It's not that I don't have any other options, but out of all my friends and family, Ryan knows me the best.

What we've been through this year has made us close. I think I can safely say he's turned into my best friend somewhere in the last six months.

As I wait, images of what was happening on my bed flash though my head. I guess I should have seen it coming, really. A leopard never changes it spots, right?

Eventually, the tears come flooding out. To add to my misery, I now have black mascara streaks running down my cheeks and red puffy eyes.

Finally, I see headlights coming my way and Ryan's white Honda Civic pulling into his drive. At first, he looks shocked to see me. That changes to anger as he strides towards me.

Ryan

AS I COME TO A STOP, I can see that there's a very wet Molly huddled in my porch. She looks dreadful. I come to a very quick conclusion that it's because of her dickhead of a boyfriend. I knew it was coming; it was just a matter of when.

"Ryan," Molly sobs as I lift her tiny frame off the ground and into a hug. She shakes from both the cold and the sobs wracking her body.

Tucking her into my side, I grab her bags and let us in. On the ground floor, my townhouse has a large room with French doors looking out to the courtyard garden, and a bathroom. I thought it would make an excellent gym. The middle floor is an open-plan kitchen, living, and dining room with a small cloakroom, and the top floor has three bedrooms, one being the master with ensuite and the other a large family bathroom.

I love it.

From the moment I looked at the plans, I just knew it was going to be my little piece of heaven, and I'm still in awe that I was able to buy this place. I'll be forever grateful for the generous gift from Susan and Pete. Nothing will ever make up for what we all lost, but thanks to them, I've been able to attempt to move on with my life.

Currently, there are boxes everywhere. I haven't had much time to unpack with everything I had to do at school to end the year, but my first holiday job is to get this place sorted and looking like a home.

Anger fills my veins as I lead us up to the living room. "It's going to be okay. Let's get you warm and dry and you can tell me what the fucker did." My fists clench. I want to beat the shit out of him for treating her so badly for so long.

"How do you know he's done anything?" Molly asks in a quiet voice.

"I can read you like a book, Molly Carter. Plus, he's a massive dickhead. I think I've mentioned that before. Only Max can make you feel this bad about yourself."

"Why was I so fucking stupid? I had my doubts, everyone had their doubts, but he convinced me that it was what he wanted. I'm not really surprised, but what does shock me is how much it *hurts*."

"Come on, get your arse upstairs and in the shower. I'll find you a t-shirt to wear."

AS I ROOT through a suitcase in one of the spare bedrooms, the door to my ensuite shuts. I pull out my Oxford Brookes polo and leave it on my bed. I hope my choice will make her smile, remembering happier times.

I knock lightly on the door. "Have you got everything you need?"

There's silence for a few seconds, and I can imagine her checking out all the products in the shower, realising they're all for men. Eventually, I hear a quiet "Yes" from the other side of the door.

"Okay, I'll see you downstairs when you're done. Take your time."

I gather up her wet clothes and take them with me. They may be soaked, but I can still smell her vanilla scent on them. It makes me feel oddly warm inside. She's been my rock for the past six months. I don't know what I would have done without her.

As I put everything in the washing machine, I spot her bra poking out of the pile. "What the fuck do I do with this?" I mutter to myself. Something in me wonders if it needs some kind of special cycle in the machine, but fuck if I know. I decide to shove it all in and just put it on a cool, quick wash.

That shouldn't do it much damage, right?

DOWNLOAD NOW to continue reading

Printed in Poland
by Amazon Fulfillment
Poland Sp. z o.o., Wrocław